THE MILLION DOLLAR PUTT

DAN GUTMAN

Hyperion Paperbacks for Children

New York

First Hyperion Paperbacks edition, 2007
3 5 7 9 10 8 6 4
Printed in the United States of America
This book is set in Century Expanded
Library of Congress Cataloging-in-Publication Data on file.
ISBN-13: 978-0-7868-3642-0
ISBN-10: 0-7868-3642-3 (pbk.)
Visit www.hyperionbooksforchildren.com

ACKNOWLEDGMENTS

Thanks to Gil Kayson, Norman Kritz, and James Ganter of the
Middle Atlantic Blind Golf Association;
the Overbrook School for the Blind in Philadelphia;
and the generous help of Lisa O'Malley, Jude Ogleman,
Brian Mackey, Steve Butler, Robert Pallies,
Nina Wallace, Irv Klubeck, Lacey Chemsak,
Donna Bray, and all the folks at Hyperion.

CHAPTER 1

Just a Putt

"IT'S JUST A PUTT. Nothin' but a little putt."

Yeah, and King Kong was nothin' but a little monkey.

It was nothin' but a little *life or death* putt. Nothin' but the most important putt I would ever take. Nothin' but a freaking *million dollar putt*!

Think of it—most people work their whole life and never earn a million bucks. All I had to do was roll a stupid little white ball into a hole and I'd be rich. Funny how things work out sometimes.

If I missed, of course, I'd get a handshake and a

sympathetic pat on the back. Nothing. Nada. Zip. Bupkes.

That's what I like about sports. You win or you lose. There's no in-between. The real world is a complicated, confusing mess of gray. That's what Birdie Andrews always tells me. Sports makes it simple. Black or white. On or off. Somebody goes home happy, and somebody goes home heartbroken. If only the real world were as simple as that.

Hitting a golf ball is such a strange thing, when you think about it. Some kids can whack it two hundred yards right down the middle of the fairway. But you put a putter in their hands and they turn to jelly. Can't do it. Too much pressure. Other kids putt like a laser beam, but they can't hit the ball off a tee fifty yards.

Putting may be the hardest part of the game. The thing is, it *seems* like it should be so easy. It doesn't take any strength. You tap the ball. It's almost like playing roly-poly. Piece of cake. Anybody can do it.

A golf ball is 1.68 inches wide. Yeah, I measured. The hole is 4.25 inches wide. How can anyone miss? But we do. Most of the time, in fact, we miss any putt longer than three feet.

Golfers go nutty over putting. I've heard of people who missed a crucial putt and broke their putter over their knee in frustration. Or they chuck it into a pond and give up golf forever.

I was looking at a ten-foot putt. Not easy, but definitely makeable. If I sink it, I'm an instant millionaire and I win the Greater Hawai'i Under Fifteen Golf Tournament. Miss it, and chances are I finish second. Not that there's anything wrong with second place, of course. It's better than third. But first place is better. A million bucks is better than a dollar fifty, which is what I have in my wallet right now. Big trophies are better than little ones. I want the trophy that's taller than I am. I want the check with all those zeros on it.

It's not like this was important. It's not like it was the shot of a lifetime or anything. No, it was bigger than that. Let me put it this way—I REALLY WANTED TO WIN!

I walked around the green to get a feel for it. The most important thing is to figure out if the ball is going to break to the left or right, and how much. That's key. Sometimes it's easy to tell. Sometimes it's impossible. Then you just have to hit the ball straight at the hole and hope for the best.

It seemed like there was a slight break to the right. So I would have to hit the ball a few inches to the left of the hole and let the slope of the green and gravity carry it into the hole.

There was also a slight downhill slope between the ball and the hole. I could feel it in my shoes. My weight shifted slightly to the back when I stood up straight. I would have to hit the ball a little bit gentler to make sure it didn't bump right over the hole.

At the same time, I told myself, make sure you hit it hard enough. If you don't hit it hard enough, it's not going to go in even if you line it up perfectly. You don't want to leave it short. At least if you hit it a little too hard, you still have a chance.

So many things to think about. I walked back to the ball.

"No pressure, Bogie!" somebody cracked as I got myself in position. The crowd on both sides laughed. I was dead serious.

Wind wasn't a factor. Sometimes it can be when you're putting, but not today. I could barely feel the Kona breeze blowing in from the southwest.

I got myself set. Photographers were clicking away on my left and right. I tried to ignore them. People were whispering to each other as if I couldn't hear them. I heard every word.

Forget about the money, I told myself. Treat it like

any other putt. But I couldn't. A million bucks would buy a lot of guitar strings. A million bucks would buy a lot of *anything*. It was my money to win.

I took a deep breath and held it. Then I let it out slowly.

"Okay," I finally muttered to myself, "let's do this."

I took my stance and concentrated on what I needed to do. Head down. Smooth stroke. Firm follow-through. No hesitation. Just the way Birdie told me to do it.

A little boy off to the right was distracting me. I heard him tell his mother he had to go to the bathroom.

"Quiet!" the kid's mother said. "The blind kid is about to putt for a million dollars!"

CHAPTER 2

Nobody's Perfect

LET ME BACK up a little. You wanna hear a blind joke?

This lady is taking a bath when her doorbell rings.

"Who is it?" she yells.

"Blind man," a guy replies.

"I'll be right there," the lady says.

She climbs out of the bathtub. Because it's a blind man, she figures there's no need to put on any clothes. Stark naked, she opens the door.

"Hi," the guy says. "Where do you want me to put these venetian blinds?"

* * *

Okay, so it's not the funniest joke in the world. Give me a break, will ya? There aren't that many funny jokes about blind people.

I'm not *totally* blind. I can tell the difference between light and dark. I can tell when it's daytime, and I can see some color a few inches away. But that's about it. For me, it's like looking at the world through translucent glass all the time.

I have this thing called retinitis pigmentosa. RP, for short. I'm not going to bore you with the details. Basically, RP destroys the rods and cones of your retina, which is sort of the film in the camera that is your eye. Or the microchip in a digital camera.

RP happens gradually over time. At first, you find that you have trouble seeing at night. Then you lose your peripheral vision, which is your sight out of the corners of your eyes. Finally, your field of view narrows. Some people with RP become totally blind.

I was lucky, I guess. I could see perfectly well until I was about three years old. By the time I was four, I was pretty much blind. Every so often I'll have a vague flashback and remember what something looked like when I was really little. I know what the color blue looks like. To some people who were blind from birth, colors are meaningless. They can't even understand the idea of things being different colors.

RP is hereditary. That means it's in your genes. There's no cure. Some doctors think that taking high doses of vitamin A slows it down. I take a lot of vitamin A. I eat a lot of carrots, too. They're good for your eyes, right? Ever see a rabbit wearing glasses? Can't hurt, I figure.

Anyway, we deal with what we're given. Some kids have ADHD or learning disabilities. Some kids can't do math. Some kids are real short, or tall, or fat, or whatever. Everybody's got something weird about them. It sucks being blind, of course, but there are a lot of suckier things that can happen to a kid. Like getting run over by a train, for instance. That would totally suck.

Hey, you want to hear another blind joke?

Why don't blind people skydive?

Because it scares the heck out of the dog.

Oh, come on! You've gotta admit that's funny.

When I told that joke at school one day, the kids weren't sure if it was okay to laugh. Sighted kids never know how to act around blind kids like me. They're never sure if they should treat us special or not. Should you help us cross the street? Should you open the door for us? Should you tell us when we're about to smash into something? Should you feel sorry for us, or not? Maybe we'll be offended no matter what you do.

That's probably why the kids at school pretty much act like I'm a freak and ignore me. I guess I make them feel uneasy or uncomfortable or something. Sometimes I wish there was another blind kid at my school. But it's okay, I like being by myself.

People are usually surprised to find out that I'm good at things. Sports and stuff. Like, they think a blind kid must be some spaz who has funny-looking eyes and bumps into walls all the time.

Before I started playing golf, I spent most of my time playing guitar. Never took a lesson. I just picked up a guitar one day in a music store and everything came naturally to me.

I've got a Martin Hawaiian X guitar with a graphite bridge and bow-tie plate. I got it cheap at a flea market in Hilo, which is on the other side of the island. The guitar has a sweet tone. I also have an old Yamaha that was my first guitar.

I play anything. Rock. Flamenco. Folk. Slack-key. Classical, even. I like the blues, but I don't like to play them when people are around. Too many blind guys play the blues. Blind Lemon Jefferson. Blind Willie McTell. Blind Blake. It looks like a stereotype.

My favorite place to play guitar is up in the candlenut tree in my backyard. There's a thick branch about eight feet off the ground. My dad hammered some pieces of wood into the trunk so I could climb up there.

That was how I met Birdie Andrews the first time. I was sitting up in the tree with my Yamaha after school. It was a nice day, and I was just enjoying being outside, listening to the birds and all that. They inspired me. I was playing "Blackbird," an old song by the Beatles. It's a cool song, because you slide your fingers all the way up from the second fret to the eleventh. It's really simple to play, but it makes you sound like you're a great guitar player.

So I'm up there playing in the tree, and suddenly something jumped on my arm. Maybe it was a mongoose or a gecko or one of those giant cockroaches you only find in Hawai'i.

Whatever it was, it startled me. I flinched. And to make a long story short, well, I fell out of the tree.

CHAPTER 3

The Day I Met Birdie

I'LL ALWAYS remember my first conversation with Birdie Andrews. . . .

Birdie: Ohmygod!

Me: What happened?

Birdie: You fell out of the tree! Are you okay?

Me: I think so. My guitar is pretty busted up, though.

Birdie: You landed on top of it. Maybe I can fix it.

She had a nice voice. It was almost musical.

Me: Who are you?

Birdie: Bird. Bird Andrews.

Me: Bird? That's your real name?

Birdie: My parents are sort of nuts. They're into birds in a big way. Most people call me Birdie. What's your name?

Me: Ed. Ed Bogard. Most people call me Bogie. Hey, Birdie and Bogie, get it?

Birdie: Get what?

Me: Birdie and Bogie. They're both golf terms.

Birdie: Oh. I never played golf.

Me: Neither have I. But I know that a birdie is when you take one stroke less than par, and a bogey is when you take one stroke more than par.

Birdie: What's par?

Me: Never mind. How old are you?

Birdie: Thirteen.

Me: Me too. Do you go to Waikoloa School?

Birdie: No, my parents send me to Waimea. It's an artsy-fartsy private school in Kona.

Me: Are you artsy-fartsy?

Birdie: Not particularly. I do a little sculpting.

It occurred to me that this girl Birdie got to me about a second after I hit the ground.

Me: Hey, how did you know I fell out of the tree?

Birdie: I was watching you.

Me: Watching me? For how long?

Birdie: About a year. Ever since we moved in next door.

Me: You've been watching me for a year and you never said anything? What are you, some kind of a stalker?

Birdie: No! I just . . . didn't want you to know I was watching.

Me: Don't you have anything better to do than watch me?

Birdie: Not really. I like to listen to you play. It's like a free concert every day. Y'know, there's a talent show at my school every year. You should be in it. You're really good.

Me: I don't think so.

The fact is, I never liked performing in front of people. I did it a few times. When there are people watching me play guitar, I start sweating like crazy. Stage fright, I guess.

Birdie: Is it hard to play when you're blind? How do you know where to put your fingers?

Sighted people think blind kids can't do anything. Either that, or they think we have supernatural powers.

Me: Blind people can do anything sighted people can do. Except drive, I guess. Playing guitar is easy. I'll teach you some chords if you want.

Birdie: Oh, I wouldn't be any good.

Me: How do you know? Everybody's good at something.

Birdie: What's it like to be blind? Ohmygod, I'm sorry. I wasn't supposed to ask that. You don't like it when people ask that, do you?

Me: "You"? You mean, blind people? Like we're all one person? Some of us do. Some of us don't. How do you know what I like or don't like?

Birdie: You made a face when I asked you what it's like to be blind.

Me: It's just that I get asked that question a lot. What would you say if people constantly asked you what it's like to *see*?

Birdie: I don't know. I'd say I open my eyes, and there it is.

Me: Well, I open my eyes and there it's not.

I told her a little bit about RP and she peppered me with questions. It was annoying explaining it for the five-thousandth time, but it was nice that she was interested. Some people don't even care. It was also nice to have some company. And I hadn't met a lot of girls my age.

I wondered what Birdie looked like. Usually, when I meet a new person, I take a guess about what they look like. I'm usually way off. But based on her voice, I imagined Birdie to be tall, skinny, with long hair, probably brown. As long as she was getting all personal, I figured I could get personal, too.

Me: Hey, what do you look like?

Birdie: I'm a horrible, deformed monster. I have a hunchback and two noses.

Me: You're goofing on me.

I tried to touch her face, but she pushed my hand away.

Birdie: Hey, get your paws off me, you perv! I don't even know you!

Me: Sorry!

Birdie: I'm just kidding. Go ahead, touch my face if you want.

I reached out and touched her face, her ears, her nose, and her hair. Everything seemed to be in order. Her hair was long. Her skin was soft. Her mouth was smiling. She giggled when I felt the braces on her teeth.

Me: Something tells me you don't look like a monster. What color hair do you have?

Birdie: What difference does it make? Beauty is only skin-deep. Isn't that what they say? Why does it matter what I look like?

I wasn't sure if she meant looks shouldn't matter in general, or if she meant looks shouldn't matter because I can't see anyway. I let it pass.

Me: You have an accent. I can't place it. Boston?

Birdie: Close. Maine.

Me: Why did you move all the way to Hawai'i?

Birdie: My parents are birders. You know, bird-watchers.

Me: Did they run out of birds to watch in Maine?

Birdie: Look, I don't want to talk about it.

Me: You don't have to tell me.

Birdie: I had . . . it's personal.

Me: I'm sorry I brought it up.

Birdie: It's okay. How come I never see your mom around?

Me: It's personal.

Birdie: You're right. It's none of my business.

Me: My mom is dead.

I was telling her way too much. I never tell anybody about my mother. I didn't know why I was opening up to this complete stranger.

Birdie: Oh jeez, I'm sorry. What happened?

Me: She was struck by lightning.

Birdie: You shouldn't joke about things like that.

Me: I'm not joking. My mom was struck by lightning. That's how she died.

Birdie: Ohmygod! It must have been horrible!

Me: I was four. I barely remember.

Birdie: Is your dad a scuba diver or something? I always see him carrying tanks and stuff around.

Me: He's a golf-ball diver.

Birdie: A golf-ball diver? What's that?

Me: He jumps into ponds on golf courses and fishes out the balls people hit in there.

Birdie: You're joking, right?

Me: No. For real. Then he sells the balls. That's his business. He'll pull out a thousand golf balls in a day. Even more, sometimes.

Birdie: Wow!

We had one of those awkward pauses when neither person has anything to say and you quickly try to think of something. Silence is okay when you know somebody well, but for some reason when you're getting to know somebody, it's just weird when nobody is talking. I tried desperately to think of something to say.

Me: So what bands are you into?

Birdie: I'm not into bands.

Me: You're a bookworm, then?

Birdie: I'm not that into books either.

Me: So what are you into?

Birdie: You really want to know?

Me: Yeah.

Birdie took my hand.

CHAPTER 4

Shrinking the World

USUALLY WHEN people lead me somewhere, they put a hand on my elbow to guide me. But Birdie took my hand in her hand and led me across my backyard, down some steps, and over a gravel driveway. I hadn't held hands with a girl since second grade. It was nice.

Birdie and I live in Waikoloa Village, which is on the island of Hawai'i. It's called the Big Island, but it's only a little bigger than Connecticut. The Big Island is actually five volcanoes sort of fused together, and some are active. One of them, Mauna Loa, erupted in 1985.

They call Kilauea a "drive-in volcano" because you can actually watch the bubbling lava from your car. Pretty cool.

You probably think Mount Everest is the highest mountain in the world. But we have a mountain called Mauna Kea that's even higher—if you measure it from the base of the ocean floor. We also have Hi'ilawe Falls, the highest waterfall in the islands.

They say the Big Island is so pretty that it hurts your eyes. It figures that I live in the most beautiful place on earth, and I can't see it.

Anyway, I had been living in Waikoloa for my whole life, but I didn't know that Birdie had been living next door for the last year.

"Careful," she said, pulling open her screen door. "We're going around this corner and then down the steps."

"Is this okay with your parents?" I asked.

"They're hardly ever home," she replied. "They're always out birding."

The bottom of the steps had the musty smell of a basement. There wasn't stuff all over the place, like in my basement. Still, I hadn't gone five steps when I bumped into something hard. Birdie apologized and told me it was an air hockey table. She led me to another table at the other end of the basement.

"Climb up," she said.

"What for?"

"You'll see."

"No I won't."

I climbed up on the table, being careful to feel in front of me so I would know where the edge was.

"What is it?" I asked.

"Guess," Birdie replied, giggling.

I felt all around the table. It was some kind of a giant model. The surface was bumpy, like one of those globes where the mountains pop up off the earth. I could feel some little trees too, and roads, and some tiny buildings.

"It's a map of some sort," I said.

"A map of what?" Birdie asked, still giggling.

I felt around some more. There were eight big bumps that came up out of what I figured was supposed to be water.

"Is it Hawai'i?" I guessed. There are eight major Hawaiian islands.

"Very good!" Birdie said, clapping her hands.

Now I could tell exactly what it was. I could feel the shape of the Big Island, Oahu, Maui, Lanai, Kauai, Molokai, Kahoolawe, and Niihau. The peaks of Mauna Loa and Mauna Kea poked up off the table.

There were the big hotels in Honolulu. The detail was incredible.

"You built this all by yourself?" I asked.

"Sculpting is just a hobby."

"I thought you said you weren't good at anything," I said.

"It's a useless skill," she replied. "A waste of time, really."

"Then why do you do it?"

Birdie paused for a moment.

"The real world is so big," she said. "I like the idea of shrinking things down. You know, to make stuff simple? It makes me feel more in control."

"So you built a miniature world." I said.

Most of the girls in my school, all they ever talk about is clothes, how much they weigh, what dumb TV show they like, and which guys are cute. Stupid stuff like that. Birdie was different, that was for sure.

"Your world is smaller, self-contained," she said. "Sometimes I wish I could eliminate one of my senses."

"Yeah, being blind for life is really *great*," I said sarcastically. "Too bad only a few of us get to enjoy this wonderful experience."

"Very funny," she said. "I went in an isolation tank once. Have you ever done that? They put you in a tank filled with warm salt water. There's no sound, no light, no stimulation. You just float. I started hallucinating. It was awesome. You should try it."

This chick was twisted. It was getting just a little too weird for me.

"Hey, how about a game of air hockey?" I suggested.

"I don't like games," Birdie said. "Competition brings out the worst in people."

"Come on, 'fraid you'll lose to a blind kid?"

"How can you play air hockey if you can't see?" she asked.

"Like I told you, I can do anything except drive," I said. "Come on, chicken, I'll go easy on you."

I found the round thing you hold in your hand. Birdie found a puck and pushed the button to turn the table on. I could hear the air coming out of the little holes on the surface, and feel it on the palm of my hand.

"You can go first," she said, sliding the puck until it bounced near the goal I was defending. "First one to score six goals wins."

"Winner takes out," I called.

I put the puck in the middle of the table and whacked it off the left side. It clattered into her goal. 1–0.

"Hey, I wasn't ready!" Birdie complained.

"You snooze, you lose," I said. "Get ready for this one."

She slid the puck to me again. This time I faked hitting it to the left and smacked it off the right side instead. It clattered into the goal. 2–0.

What can I say? I have a knack for physical stuff. Either that, or Birdie really sucked at air hockey.

I missed the next shot, but I kept my paddle right in front of the goal and blocked her return shot. We had a little back-and-forth action and then she slipped the puck past me for a goal. 2–1.

"Yeah!" Birdie yelled.

Okay, no more Mr. Nice Guy. I concentrated on the sound of the puck, being careful not to let my hand stray more than a few inches away from the goal I was defending. I got another shot by her and followed it up with another one on the serve. 4–1.

"Hey, you're good!" she said.

I wondered if she was letting me win. That's what people do sometimes with blind kids. They think they'll make you feel good if they let you win. Turns out you feel worse because you know you didn't earn it. But I didn't think Birdie was letting me win. She was grunting and yelling and cursing with each shot. For somebody who didn't like competition, she was trying really hard.

She scored a couple of more goals on me, but then she accidentally knocked one into her own goal to make it 5–3.

"Point game," I said.

"You're going *down*," she warned.

"Oh, I don't *think* so," I said, putting the puck in the middle. Across the table, I could hear Birdie panting. How do you get winded playing air hockey?

I faked hitting it to the left. Then I faked hitting it to the right. Then I faked left again. Then I whacked it off the right side and the puck clattered into the goal. 6–3. A little bell rang. Victory is sweet!

"I *told* you I wasn't good at anything," she said, pounding the table with her fist. "I hate games."

No she didn't. It was losing that she hated. I should have let her win, but it occurred to me too late. That would have been the right thing to do. Some people can't handle losing, and losing to a blind kid must be even harder to deal with.

"I'd better go," I said.

Birdie walked me back up the steps and across the driveway. I told her I could take it from there.

"How do you know how to get to your house from here?" she asked.

"There are eighteen steps between this spot and my back door," I said.

I had learned a lot about Birdie in a very short period of time. People would say Birdie Andrews is a little odd. People would be right. She'd learned a lot about me too.

"Anything else I can do for you?" she asked before heading back to her house.

"Yeah," I said. "Next time you're spying on me, come over and say aloha."

"Okay," she said. "*A hui hou aku.*"

That means, "Good-bye until we meet again."

CHAPTER 5
Jerks and Morons

I DIDN'T THINK much about Birdie Andrews over the next couple of days. I had homework and projects and a math test to study for. But while I was sitting in social studies, I suddenly remembered my busted Yamaha, which must have still been sitting under the candlenut tree in the backyard. Luckily, it hadn't rained. I made a note on my digital recorder to remind me to pick up the guitar after school.

Back before the days of computers, it must have been a lot tougher for blind kids in school. Braille was pretty much the only way to read or write, and Braille is really hard to learn. I never mastered it myself. I didn't have to. I've got a computer with a scanner and a built-in speech synthesizer. So when I type, scan, or download text into it, it can take the words and speak them to me so I can hear them. There are also plenty of books on CD now. A lot of blind kids don't learn Braille these days.

"Pssst, hey, Bogie!"

I recognized the voice. It was Hunter Lynch, this kid in my homeroom. He threw his arm around my shoulder as I was walking into the class. I switched my cane to the other hand so I wouldn't bump my elbow into him.

"I gotta tell you a secret," Hunter whispered. "You know Emily Lapakahi?"

"Yeah," I said.

"She digs you."

"How do you know?" I said, finding my desk and putting my backpack underneath. I was a few minutes early. Our homeroom teacher, Mrs. Harmon, probably wasn't there yet.

"Emily asked me to ask you if you'll go out with her," Hunter told me.

"Why doesn't she talk to me herself?" I asked.

"She's shy, man. She's afraid it'll look bad if you say

no. That's why she asked me to be the go-between. What do you say?"

I hadn't talked much with Emily Lapakahi. She was a really smart girl who had a squeaky voice. I remembered back in third grade we had to do oral reports and dress up like a famous Hawaiian. Emily did King Kalakaua, who wrote the Hawaiian national anthem before we were part of the United States.

"I'll think about it," I said.

"She wants an answer now, man," said Hunter. "Emily is really cute, Bogie. Don't pass up this chance. She really likes you. Man, I wish she liked me. I have such a crush on her. Some guys have all the luck. Come on, I'll take you over to her."

I listened. They say that because we can't see, our other senses become more sensitive. I pick up signals like a satellite dish. I hear *everything*. I can detect a whisper from across the room. It just comes naturally.

It's strange, because a lot of sighted kids assume that because I can't see, I can't hear either. In fact, I hear better than they do. So I listened hard.

That's when I heard what I was listening for—giggling. Snickering.

It was Hunter's posse of jerks—Ronnie, Alex, and Jonah—who were probably standing right behind him the whole time. I know a setup when I hear one.

Emily was probably the ugliest girl in the school. She probably had giant buck teeth, or terminal acne. I felt sorry for her. But that didn't mean I wanted to go out with her.

I could have just laughed it off and been a good sport. Jerks play practical jokes on blind kids all the time. I can take it. You get used to it. But I didn't want to be a good sport. Not with Hunter Lynch.

"Okay," I said, "take me over to Emily."

He put his arm on my elbow and walked me over to the other side of the room.

"Hey, Emily—" Hunter began, but I jumped in.

"Emily," I said, "I have something to tell you."

"What is it?" she asked, in that squeaky voice.

"Hunter just told me that he has a crush on you, and he's too shy to tell you himself. Do you want to go out with him?"

"I didn't say that!" Hunter shouted.

"Oooooh!" everybody said.

"Hunter likes Emily!" somebody said.

"He's lying!" Hunter shouted.

"You're both jerks!" said Emily, and she stomped away while everybody went *oooooh* again.

I felt bad about doing that to Emily. I just couldn't

resist sticking it to Hunter. His posse was laughing out loud now, and they were laughing at *him*.

"Ooh, Bogie totally gave it back to you, man!" Alex said.

"You got flipped by a blind kid!" said Ronnie.

"He zinged you big-time, Hunter!" Jonah said.

"Shut up!" Hunter told them.

Jerk.

I know it's wrong to stereotype people. But this guy is a jerk. Hunter is one of these guys who gets pleasure out of humiliating other people. Every so often he'll put a chair in front of me when I'm walking, or sneak up behind me and yell "BOO" in my ear to startle me. I've heard him call me "Special Ed" when he thought I couldn't hear him. If he dropped dead tomorrow, I wouldn't care. The world would be a better place.

Some blind kids go to schools for the blind so they won't have to deal with jerks like Hunter. There's no school for the blind around here, so I go to public school. I'm not sure I would go to a school for blind kids even if there were one.

Not that I have anything against those schools. But just because you go to a special school doesn't mean kids won't make fun of you. Some kids are just jerks, whether they have sight or not. If they can't make fun of the way you look, they'll make fun of the way you talk, the things you do, the way you smell, or whatever. Jerks seem to always be able to find something to be jerky about.

Hunter Lynch isn't in any of my regular classes, but at the end of the day he and his brain-dead flunkies are in my study skills class. That's just a class where we can make sure we have what we need to bring home or ask a teacher a question—stuff like that.

I was trying to get a jump on my homework, but Hunter, Ronnie, Jonah, and Alex were talking, so it was hard to concentrate.

They were talking about sports, which is the only subject they seem to know anything about. They had all been in some soccer game over the weekend.

"Man, you guys really stunk on Saturday," Hunter told the others.

"Not as bad as you guys stunk," Jonah said.

"Oh, you stink too," Alex said.

That's about as clever as Hunter and his pals get. I guess they got tired of goofing on each other, so they started yanking my crank.

"Hey, Bogie," Hunter said. "Are there any sports blind people play?"

"Yeah," I said, "I totally rule at Pin the Tail on the Donkey."

The four of them combined have the IQ of one normal person, and they didn't even get it for about three seconds. Then they all started cackling and congratulating me like I had made the funniest joke in the world.

Morons.

The fact is, I'm good at sports. My dad was an athlete in high school and college, and he'd taken me waterskiing, kayaking, and holua sledding (that's when you race down a steep mountain course on a wooden sled). People are always amazed when they see a blind kid on water skis or whatever, but it's really no big deal. Just because you're blind doesn't mean you aren't physically coordinated. I didn't bother telling Hunter and company. They'd probably never believe me anyway.

"Hey," said Hunter. "How about we go over to Swing Zone and bang out a bucket of golf balls after school?"

"I'm in," said Jonah.

"I'm grounded," Alex said. "My mom got all psycho because I got a D on the last math test."

"I'll go," said Ronnie. "I have birthday money to spend."

Waikoloa is practically the golf capital of the world. There are ten golf courses within about a half hour of each other. People here are golf crazy, and golfers come from all over the world to play here. Bad golfers. That's why my dad can dig a thousand balls a day out of the ponds.

"Hey, Bogie," Hunter said. "Wanna come to Swing Zone with us?"

"He's blind, you dork!" said Alex. "He can't play golf."

"I know!"

"Maybe he'd like to *hear* us play," Ronnie said. A couple of them snickered.

I thought about it. They were jerks, of course. They were the last people in the world that I would ever want to hang out with. But I always wanted to try golf. I had asked my dad to take me golfing a million times. He always said no. He took me windsurfing. He took me hang gliding. He took me Snuba diving (that's a combination of scuba and snorkeling. You breathe through a long hose attached to an air tank that's floating on a raft). But he wouldn't take me golfing for some reason.

I look at it this way. I'm just about useless at sports where the ball is moving. I couldn't hit a baseball or a tennis ball or a soccer ball. But golf is a sport where the ball doesn't move until *after* you hit it. The ball just sits there. How hard could it be?

"Sure," I said. "I'll go."

CHAPTER 6

Too Many Friends

WHEN I GOT off the bus after school, Dad was in the kitchen scrubbing golf balls. Every day he gets up before six o'clock in the morning, puts on his scuba gear, and goes diving for balls. Or, as he calls them, sunken treasure.

I would tell you what my dad looks like, but it wouldn't be a very good description because I barely remember. He's a big man, I know that, with a deep voice. He wears a baseball cap most of the time. Sometimes I can smell that pond scum on him if he doesn't take a really good shower at the end of the day.

Diving for golf balls is only part of his work. The more important (and not very exciting) part is sorting the balls he finds. At the end of the day, he takes all the balls in his nets and washes them in a big bucket of chlorine. Then he scrubs them with a brush. I usually help if I don't have too much homework.

Once the balls are clean, he has to sort them. You see, a beat-up, junky old ball with marks or cuts on it that's been under water for a month is worth about a quarter or even less. But a clean, white Titleist Pro V1 will go for three dollars. Dad calls those white gold. He sorts the balls into twelve grades, depending on their condition and brand. I can't help with the sorting very much, because you've got to be able to see the brand names.

Dad says that when he's under water, he can't see much better than I can. There's so much mud, crud, and who knows what down there, he can barely see a few inches in front of his mask. He has to feel his way around.

Every so often he'll come across a watch that flew off somebody's arm, or a golf club. One time he even found a whole golf cart somebody must have driven into the pond.

"Hey, I had me a little run-in with an alligator

today," Dad told me when I put my backpack on the counter.

"What happened?"

"I came up to the surface with a net full of balls and there he was, two feet away, staring me in the face with those big eyes."

"What did you do?" I asked.

"I smacked him in the snout with a five iron."

Golf-ball diving is not an easy job. Dad has shared ponds with snapping turtles, snakes, eels, crabs, ducks, geese, and spiny-backed catfish. Even if the wildlife isn't bothering him, he never knows when some golfer is going to whack a ball into the pond and bonk him on the head with it. Drowning is a possibility, too. Every so often a golf-ball diver will panic after being weighed down too much with the balls and scuba stuff. What a sucky way to die.

But on a good day, Dad says, diving for golf balls is like playing Pac-Man. He finds a spot and just keeps scooping up those little white dots. After eight hours of work, his truck is filled with balls. There must be a lot of golfers out there whacking balls into ponds. And they spend a lot of money buying back those same balls, over and over again. It's another form of recycling.

"You got homework, Ed?" Dad asked. He's probably the only person I know who doesn't call me Bogie.

"I'll do it later," I said. "Some guys from school are coming over."

"Oh, yeah?"

"They're taking me to Swing Zone."

I tried to sound casual about it, but I knew immediately that Dad had stopped scrubbing golf balls and was staring at me. For a guy whose whole life revolves around golf, he really hates the game. He doesn't play, and he never wants me to play.

"Swing Zone. That place in Kona?" he asked. "Why do you want to go there?"

"To hit some golf balls."

"They're gonna make fun of you, you know," Dad said. "Can't you see that? Let's take the blind kid out to the driving range and have a few laughs. That's what they're saying to each other. You don't need that."

"You always complain that I don't have friends," I said. "How do you expect me to make friends if I don't do stuff like this?"

"Those guys aren't gonna be your friends," Dad said.

"How do *you* know?"

He was right, of course. Hunter Lynch and his pals

were never going to be friends of mine. But I didn't want to admit that to Dad. I didn't want him telling me what to do, or not to do. That's the natural order of the universe, right? Dads tell you how you should run your life, and you tell them to leave you alone.

Dad and I argue a bit. Sometimes I think he resents me because he got stuck raising me when my mom died. After that, he had to be both my dad *and* my mom.

The doorbell rang and I went to answer it.

"I brought you something."

It wasn't Hunter's voice, as I expected. It was Birdie Andrews, the flaky girl next door.

"What is it?" I asked.

Birdie put a guitar in my hands. My Yamaha! It wasn't broken and splintered. It was in perfect condition. I strummed a chord. The guitar was even in tune.

"You fixed it all by yourself?" I asked.

"Mostly," she said. "A guy at the music store helped me with some parts."

Dad came out to the front door. I introduced him to Birdie.

"You didn't have to do this," I told her.

"If we only did things we had to do, it would be a really dull world," Birdie replied.

"Here, let me give you some money," said Dad. "It's the least—"

"No, really, thanks anyway," Birdie said. "But I'd love to hear you play some more, Bogie. I like that song you were playing the other day."

"I can't right now," I said. "Some guys are about to pick me up. We're going to go hit golf balls."

"I thought you told me you never played golf," Birdie said.

"This'll be the first time," I explained.

"Oh."

I could hear the disappointment in her voice. After going so long with nobody my age to hang out with, suddenly I had too many friends.

"I don't like the idea either," Dad said.

That's when it clicked—this girl Birdie *liked* me. She wouldn't have repaired my Yamaha if she didn't like me. She wouldn't come over to hear me play if she didn't like me. And she wouldn't be jealous of those guys if she didn't like me.

Out on the street, a car horn honked.

"Hey, Bogie!" Hunter yelled. "Let's go! Swing Zone awaits!"

"I'm coming!"

I thanked Birdie for fixing my Yamaha and

promised I'd play guitar for her some other time.

"You're going to play golf with those guys?" she asked.

"Sure," I said. What's wrong with that?"

"Think how much better the world would be if people didn't compete with one another," she said. "Why can't people just have fun? Why do we have to have winners and losers?"

"You know," my dad said, "there's a system with no winners or losers. It's called communism. The problem is, it goes against human nature. Because when there are no winners, nobody tries. Everybody is just a loser."

"You should listen to my dad," I told Birdie. "He's a very smart guy."

"Let's talk about this another time," Birdie said. "Have fun playing golf with your friends."

"Take your cell phone in case there's an emergency," Dad told me.

I grabbed my cell and my cane and followed the sound of the car's rumbling engine.

CHAPTER 7

Beginner's Luck

I CLIMBED into the backseat next to Jonah and Ronnie. Hunter sat up front with his mother.

"Have you played much golf, Ed?" Hunter's mom asked me as she pulled away from the curb. It was nice of her to start a conversation with me, I guess. At least she didn't ask me what it's like to be blind.

"This will be my first time," I said.

"Well, I think you're a very brave young man."

Ugh, I hate when people say that. Some people think blind kids are brave if we can tie our shoes without help. Fighting to defend your country is brave.

Running into a burning building to save somebody's life is brave. There's nothing brave about going to a driving range to hit some golf balls.

Hunter and his idiotic friends must have been on their best behavior, because they didn't make one obnoxious comment in the car. But then, it wasn't a long ride.

Hunter's mom dropped us off at Swing Zone and told us she would pick us up at five o'clock. She opened the trunk so the boys could take out their golf clubs.

"Was that girl your girlfriend?" Hunter asked as soon as his mom drove away.

"What girl?"

"The girl who was leaving your house when we pulled up," Hunter said.

"Oh, she lives next door," I said.

"She's hot!" Hunter said.

I listened for snickers or giggles that would suggest Hunter was putting me on, but I didn't hear any. At least I knew that Birdie didn't look like some freak. If she did, the four of them would have been falling all over themselves.

"Who was that guy in the wet suit at your front door?" Jonah asked.

"That's my dad," I said. "He's a golf-ball diver."

That got a few snickers. To some people, golf-ball diving isn't much different from Dumpster diving or collecting loose change from pay phones. I ignored the snickers. If I got all worked up every time somebody made fun of me or my dad, I'd be angry all the time.

Swing Zone is pretty cool. Besides the driving range, they have baseball batting cages and arcade games. The boys led me over to a counter. Ronnie used some of his birthday money to pay for eighty balls. The guy behind the counter didn't give him the bucket. He gave Ronnie a token and told us we could get the balls out of a machine nearby. Behind me, I could hear the sound of people whacking golf balls.

"You blind, son?" the guy behind the counter asked.

I resisted the temptation to say, "No, I use this cane as a putter." Actually I use the cane partly to signal sighted people to get out of my way when I'm walking.

"Never had a blind golfer in here," the guy said. "Heard about blind golfers, but I never seen one."

"Neither have I," I said.

We went over to the machine, and Ronnie put the token in a slot. There was a deep rumbling sound as the golf balls tumbled into a basket at the bottom. These were cheap balls, I knew. My dad always sells balls in the worst condition to driving ranges.

Ronnie said he wanted to get a soda from the machine. He offered to buy one for me, but I took a dollar out of my wallet and gave it to him. I don't like people buying me stuff.

"How can you tell a one-dollar bill from a five- or a ten-dollar bill?" Jonah asked.

"I fold them differently," I explained, showing him the bills in my wallet.

"Hey, Bogie," asked Jonah, "what's it like being blind and stuff?"

Ugh. If I had a nickel for every time somebody asked what it's like to be blind, I'd be rich. You just get sick of answering it after a while. I should just print up cards and hand them out any time somebody asks. . . .

Being bLiNd is unrelenting blAcKness and despair tWenty-four hours a day. It's a horrible nightmare existence. I wouldn't recommend it. Now please leave me alone and allow me to return to my pathetic World of dArKNess.

This whole driving range thing was new to me. The

way it works is that they have a bunch of cages about ten feet wide, and they're lined up in a long row. There are nets separating the cages so you can't accidentally whack the person in the cage next to you with a ball. On the floor of each cage is a big mat that's supposed to be like grass, but it felt more like plastic to me. The mat has a tee sticking out of a hole on each side—one for right-handed golfers, and one for lefties like me.

Jonah told me that out in the grassy field in front of the cages are a series of signs that let you know how far you hit the ball—50, 100, 150, 200, 250, and 300 yards. Hardly anybody can reach 300 yards, not even the pros.

Hunter suggested we make things "interesting" by each putting up five dollars. Whoever hit the longest drive would get to keep all the money. Jonah didn't want to bet, because he said Hunter always hits the longest ball. Hunter called him a chicken and a wuss, so Jonah chipped in the five dollars.

"Bogie," Hunter said, "you don't have to chip in because . . . it's your first time and all."

I peeled off a five-dollar bill and gave it to him, resisting my temptation to tell him to stick it where the sun don't shine.

Ronnie paid for the balls, so he got to hit first. The rest of us sat on a bench at the back of the cage.

"You might as well give me the twenty bucks now, boys," Ronnie said as he stepped up to the tee, "because I'm going deep."

Ronnie took his first swing, and Hunter and Jonah just about collapsed laughing.

"Topped it!" Ronnie grunted.

"Nice shot, Ronnie!" said Jonah. "I think that one might have gone thirty-five yards on the ground."

"The snakes are petrified now," cracked Hunter.

Ronnie quickly took another ball and teed it up. His second shot was more respectable. It went at least one hundred yards. That's the length of a football field, I thought to myself. Pretty far.

They decided that each of us would get twenty balls to hit, because there were four of us and eighty balls in the bucket. (What math geniuses!) Ronnie took his twenty shots, sometimes hitting the ball past the 100-yard marker, but mostly nicking it off to the side or popping it up in the air right in front of us.

None of them thought Ronnie was very good, not even Ronnie. But I will say one thing—I liked the *whoosh* that his golf club made as it ripped through the air. It was a beautiful sound. Listening to Ronnie swing, I could tell when he hit that "sweet spot"—the small area in the middle of the club face that sends the ball the farthest. There was a nice click. When he missed the sweet spot, it made a different sound and the ball never went very far.

They agreed that Ronnie's best shot went 150 yards, tops. He sat down on the bench and Jonah got up to take his turn.

Jonah is left-handed like me, so he used the tee on the other side of the mat. He hit the ball pretty hard, but he had a bad hook. So as soon as he hit it, the ball would veer off to the right. He tried to correct it by changing his grip and his stance, but it didn't do much good.

One of Jonah's balls reached 175 yards. Ronnie said it shouldn't count because Jonah didn't hit it straight. They argued a little, but in the end Jonah got credit for a 175-yard drive. He was winning.

"You're getting too much sidespin," Hunter explained to Jonah as he took a club out of his bag. "That's why you have that hook. Watch and learn from the master."

I could tell that Hunter was better than the others from the sound his club made when it hit the ball. He hit the sweet spot on most of his shots. A few of his drives reached 200 yards. *Two* football fields! That's a long way. I was impressed.

"This is like taking candy from a baby," Hunter said after his last shot.

Ronnie said it wasn't fair, because Hunter had been playing golf since he was four years old.

"Pay up, losers," Hunter said. "I love spending other people's money."

"What about me?" I asked.

They had almost forgotten I was there, which happens a lot with blind people. We can't see them, so they act like they can't see us either. Like we're invisible.

Jonah said I could borrow his lefty clubs. Then he handed me his driver, which is the club that hits the ball the farthest. It had a pretty big head, with horizontal grooves cut into the face. The number "1" was carved into the top. I stepped up on the mat and felt around until I found the bucket of balls. I put a ball on the little tee.

It didn't seem that different from T-ball, it occurred to me. When I was younger, I played Little League ball for a season. I could hit the ball off the tee pretty well. Then, after I hit it, one of the other kids on the team would run the bases for me.

I really liked T-ball, but the next season they played regular baseball, with the coaches doing the pitching. My coach tried to help me by telling me how high or low the ball was, but I still missed most of the time. Striking out was frustrating, so I gave up baseball. At least in golf, they don't *pitch* the ball to you.

I knew the basic grip because I had listened to a few shows on The Golf Channel on TV. Most people don't hold a golf club the way you hold a baseball bat, with two fists on top of each other. You're supposed to sort of shake hands with the club first with your right hand (if you're a lefty), and then overlap the fingers of your left hand over the thumb of your right hand. I took a practice swing.

"Watch out!" Ronnie yelled.

"Man, you almost took my head off!" Hunter shouted.

"Sorry!" I said.

"He's facing the wrong way!" Jonah said, unable to contain his laughter. Ronnie put his hands on my shoulders and turned me around.

"Oh, man, I wish I brought a camera," said Hunter, and the other guys giggled and snickered.

Hitting a golf ball was going to be harder than I thought. I couldn't tell where the ball was. Even when I ran my hand down the length of the club to estimate how long it was, it was impossible to tell how far I should stand from the ball. If I got down on my knees to find the ball, once I stood up, it was impossible to gauge where it was.

"I have an idea," Ronnie said. "I'll put the clubhead right behind the ball, okay? Then you settle into a stance."

It made sense. Ronnie put the head behind the ball and got out of the way. I relaxed my arms and adjusted my feet until I felt comfortable.

"Remember," Hunter told me, "keep your eye on the ball."

While they laughed their stupid heads off, I took a nice, easy swing. I hit something, and I was relieved at that. I knew that if I swung and missed, the three of them would probably fall off the bench in hysterics.

Actually, it sounded like I hit it pretty good. They all stopped laughing.

"Ohmygod!" Hunter said.

"What happened?" I asked.

"Straight as a bullet!" Jonah said. "Dude, you hit that ball one hundred fifty yards, easy! Ronnie, that's as far as *your* best shot!"

Hunter and Jonah were cackling like hyenas.

"Beginner's luck," Ronnie said, getting another ball. "No way you can do that again."

He put the clubhead behind the ball and I took another swing, a little harder. It felt good.

"He did it again!" Jonah said.

"He outdrove *you*, man," Ronnie said. "He's blind as a bat, and he hit the ball farther than you did."

"Shut up, Ronnie," Jonah said. "You stink anyway."

Swinging a golf club felt natural to me. The club felt like an extension of my arm. Ronnie kept setting up the balls, and with each swing I felt a little more confident. I swung the club a little harder.

I hit a few grounders and a few pop-ups, but for the most part I felt the sweet spot hitting the ball. The other guys couldn't believe it. I was hitting the ball nearly as far as Hunter. He wasn't saying much, and I had the feeling he didn't like what he was seeing.

"Let *me* try that!" he said, shoving me aside after I had hit almost all the balls.

"Don't be stupid, Hunter," Ronnie said.

"Hey, if Bogie can hit it blind, so can I," Hunter said.

"What's he doing?" I asked.

"He took off his T-shirt, and he's tying it around his head like a blindfold," Jonah said.

"Set me up, Ronnie," Hunter said. "Just like you set up Bogie."

Ronnie put a ball on the tee and Hunter's clubhead behind the ball.

"Watch this," Hunter said, and he took a swing.

He missed everything. There was just the whoosh of the club. No click. Ronnie and Jonah were hooting and hollering like it was the funniest thing they'd ever seen.

"You guys stink, you know that?" Hunter shouted.

"Any balls left?" I asked.

"Just one," Ronnie said.

"Mind if I hit it?"

"It's yours."

Ronnie set me up. Last ball. I had nothing to lose. I got myself into position and took a really good rip at it. The ball made a nice click coming off the club. I waited to hear them tell me how far it went, but none of them said anything.

"How far?" I asked.

"We don't know," Jonah said. "That sucker didn't come down yet."

"Two hundred yards . . . *plus*," Hunter finally said. "Man!"

There was more hooting and hollering.

"Bogie is like the Pinball Wizard!" Ronnie said.

"What do you mean?" asked Jonah.

"Didn't you ever hear of *Tommy*, by the Who?" Ronnie explained. "This kid named Tommy is deaf, dumb, and blind, but he can play pinball better than anybody."

I knew "Pinball Wizard." Every blind person knows the song. Ronnie started singing it, until Hunter's mom honked the horn to let us know she was there. Somebody pressed four bills into my hand. I had won the contest.

On the way home in the car, Hunter didn't say a word.

CHAPTER 8

The Natural

WHEN I GOT home from the driving range, I was whistling. I must admit, I swaggered a little when I walked up the front steps with twenty bucks in my hand. It felt *good* to have beaten Hunter Lynch. I finally got a little revenge for all the times he'd whispered behind my back, made fun of me, or moved a desk in front of me to bump into for his amusement. It gave me a surge of confidence. And I kind of enjoyed telling my dad I had hit a golf ball 200 yards.

"How do *you* know you hit a ball two hundred yards?" he asked.

"They told me I did."

"And you trust 'em?" he asked with a snort. "What makes you so sure they were telling the truth?"

"I won the contest," I said. "They gave me twenty bucks. Why would they give me their money if I hadn't hit the longest ball?"

My dad laughed.

"Ed, do you know what a hustle is?" he asked.

"No."

"It's a con job," he explained. "Here's how it works. A guy makes a bet with some sap for a small amount of money, and he loses on purpose. Then maybe he does it a few more times until the sap really thinks he's better than the guy. Then, the guy bets a much larger amount of money and this time he beats the sap and takes his money. That's a hustle. It's the oldest scam in the book. Happens all the time."

"You think they just *pretended* that I hit the longest ball so I'd play with them again?"

"Oh, yeah," Dad said. "They probably had it all planned out. Let's hustle the blind kid. Those boys are playing you for a fool."

I felt like a dork. How could I let them take advantage of me? How could I be so . . . blind?

I didn't say much over dinner. I just ate and went to my room to work on homework.

The next day at school, Hunter came over and threw his arm around me.

"Hey, that was some show you put on yesterday at the driving range," he said. "I didn't think *anybody* could hit a ball that far."

"Thanks."

"Listen," Hunter said, "how about a rematch after school tomorrow?"

"I don't think so," I told him.

No way Hunter was going to make a fool of me again. No way was he going to get that money back.

"Oh, come on," he said. "You gotta give me another chance to beat you. It's only fair."

"No rematch," I said firmly.

He took his arm off me and grabbed his books roughly.

"You humiliated me in front of my friends," Hunter said. "I'll get you back, Bogie. This isn't the end. I don't like losing."

Big man! What was he going to do to punish me, break into my house while I'm not home and rearrange the furniture?

After school that day, Birdie Andrews knocked on the door and asked if I would play guitar for her. I was still angry at Hunter. I was also angry at myself for being such a sap. I told Birdie I didn't feel like playing guitar.

"How did you do at golf yesterday?" she asked.

I told her everything. Some people are just easy to talk to. I told Birdie what happened at Swing Zone and how good I felt that I could hit a ball farther than those other guys. And I told her how bad I felt when my dad said I was being hustled.

"I know," Birdie said. "Let's go to a golf course. I'll tell you how far you hit the ball, and I'll tell you the truth."

It wasn't a bad idea. My dad was out delivering golf balls to stores, so he wouldn't have to know. The Waikoloa Village golf course was a few miles up the road. They probably had an area where I could hit a few balls.

"Do you have a bike?" I asked.

"Yeah, but I don't know how to ride," she replied.

"You don't know how to ride a bike?"

I couldn't believe it. I never heard of any kid my age who didn't know how to ride a bike.

"I told you I'm not good at things," Birdie said.

"I can teach you how to ride a bike in five minutes," I told her.

"*You* ride?" she asked.

"Sure I do," I said. "I don't go out riding by myself in the traffic or anything. But I've ridden around some big parking lots on Sunday when there are no cars there."

"Gee, I don't know. . . ." Birdie said.

"Okay, forget about riding," I said. "I'll pedal and you sit on my handlebars."

"It's too hot out."

"Oh, come on," I said. "You chicken?"

It took some convincing, but I finally talked Birdie into it. We got my bike out of the garage and I gave her my dad's helmet to put on. It's a really good idea to wear a helmet, especially when you're sitting on the handlebars of a bike being driven by a blind kid.

We rolled the bike out to the middle of Pakanu Street, and Birdie climbed on. I started pedaling. It's a lot harder to pedal with two people, but I managed. Pakanu Street is a nice, wide street with very little traffic.

"Just say go left or right if it looks like we're going to run into anything," I instructed her.

"Go left!" she screamed. "Left!"

I made a hard left and Birdie told me we missed smashing into a parked car by about six inches.

"Right!" she screamed. "Go right!"

Somebody had put one of those portable basketball backboards in the street and we nearly ran into that, too.

"I can't believe I'm doing this!" Birdie shrieked. "You're a maniac!"

After a few more near misses and potential catastrophes, we somehow made it to the parking lot of the Waikoloa Village golf course without getting killed. Birdie was out of breath, like *she* was the one who did all the pedaling.

We found the clubhouse and Birdie led me over to a desk where a guy was sitting.

"Is there a place where my friend here can hit a few golf balls?" she asked. "He's blind."

"We don't have a driving range," the guy said.

Bummer. We rode all the way over there and almost got killed—for nothing.

"Couldn't he just go out on the course for a few minutes?" Birdie said. "We won't bother anybody."

"Are you kids under fifteen?" the guy asked.

"Yeah."

"We offer a free half-hour golf lesson for kids," he said. "Would you like to take one?"

I didn't come there to take a lesson. I just wanted to hit a few balls to see if Hunter and his friends were lying to me. But hitting a few balls had to be part of the lesson, I figured.

"Sure," I said. "Sign me up."

The guy picked up his phone to call somebody, and he told us to sit down. A few minutes later, a golf cart pulled up outside and another guy came over to us.

"I'm Mr. Honalo," he said, shaking my hand. "Call me Ralph. So you want to play some golf?"

He was an old guy, I knew right away. It wasn't just his voice. It was his handshake. I can usually tell how old somebody is when I shake their hand. The skin on an old person's hand is looser. Besides, nobody names their kids Ralph anymore.

We got into the golf cart and Ralph drove us over to a practice tee, where he gives his lessons. He told us that he's been teaching golf for forty years, and that he's even taught a few other blind people. He found a left-handed club that he said was the right size for me.

"Ever swing a golf club before?" he asked.

"Once," I said. "Yesterday."

"Well, let's see what you've got."

He teed up a ball and told me he was going to position the clubhead right behind the ball, the same way Ronnie did at the driving range. I wrapped my fingers around the club and got my feet into position. Then I brought the club back and took an easy swing. I waited to hear his reaction.

"Again," was all he said.

He teed up another ball and I whacked it, just a little harder than the first one.

"Again," Ralph said.

I hit five or six balls, and then Ralph told me to stop.

"Did I do something wrong?" I asked.

"Kid," he said. "I'm sorry, but I can't teach you."

"Why not?" Birdie asked.

"He has a perfect swing," Ralph said. "Kid, you are a natural. I've never seen anything like it in all my years of teaching golf. You just hit six balls right down the middle, and each one went one hundred fifty to two hundred yards. Don't change *anything*. Don't let *anybody* fiddle with that swing. You hear me? You want my advice? My advice is, don't take any advice from *anyone*, including me. You should be entering tournaments, not taking beginner lessons."

"Oh, I could never play in a tournament," I replied. "I'd be too nervous. I just want to play for fun."

"I *knew* you would be good!" Birdie said. "Did you hear that? You have a perfect swing!"

"So, what should I do now?" I asked.

"You need to get yourself a coach," Ralph said. "A blind golfer needs somebody to help him set up for each shot, help him estimate distances, find the ball, read the green, choose the right club, tell him where the sand traps and water hazards are, all that. You need somebody to be your eyes. Blind golf is a team sport."

"Would you coach me?" I asked.

"Sure," he said. "Can you afford fifty dollars an hour?"

"What?" Birdie said. "That's outrageous!"

"I'm sorry, but that's what I charge everyone. My time is valuable."

I didn't have that kind of money, and I knew my dad wouldn't give it to me. He didn't want me playing golf in the first place.

"I can be your coach," Birdie suggested.

"You don't know squat about golf," I said.

"Neither do you," she said. "We'll learn together. You just swing. I'll be your eyes."

"But you didn't even know the difference between a birdie and a bogey," I told her.

"I know that a Birdie is offering to coach for free," she said, "and that a Bogie is a big chicken."

And that's how Birdie Andrews became my coach.

CHAPTER 9

The Blind Leading the Blind

SO I LEARNED one thing—Dad was wrong. Hunter *wasn't* hustling me at the driving range. I had beaten him fair and square.

The next day at school I went over to Hunter in homeroom. At first I was going to say I was sorry, but I really didn't have anything to apologize for. The only thing I had done was tell him I didn't want a rematch. So I didn't apologize. I just said he could have a rematch if he wanted one.

"Oh, thank you, your magnificence," he sneered. "But *I'll* decide when we have a rematch."

What a jerk. He only wanted a rematch on his own terms. What a control freak. I didn't care. I beat him. I got twenty bucks from him and his friends. He could stew as long as he wanted to.

In study skills class later that day, I went to sit in my chair. Instead, I fell on the floor. Everybody was in hysterics. The chair had been moved. I was really surprised, because I'm always careful to put a hand down on my chair before I sit on it.

When I got up and found the chair behind me, there was a string attached to one of the legs. Somebody had yanked the chair right out from under me. It had to be Hunter. What a dirtbag.

I didn't rush out to play after that golf teacher told me I had a "perfect" swing. For one thing, golf is expensive. Even with a student discount, it costs a lot of money to play a round at most golf courses. For another thing, I didn't even have golf clubs. They cost *hundreds* of dollars.

There was a third reason, too. My dad clearly didn't approve of me playing golf. I didn't know what his problem was.

So after school let out, I did what I usually did. I climbed up in the tree to play guitar. I wasn't at it very long when I heard some sounds. The sound of a chair squeaking. The sound of a page turning.

"I know you're there, Birdie," I said. "You can come out from your hiding place."

"How did you know?" she said. Her footsteps scraped across the gravel driveway. "I was trying to be so quiet."

"I have a fifth sense," I said, climbing down from my perch in the tree.

"Very funny. Hey, what's that blackbird song you keep playing?" she asked. "It's pretty."

"It's the Beatles," I told her.

"The who?"

"No, not The Who," I said. "They were a different band. Don't tell me you never heard of the Beatles."

"I never heard of the Beatles."

Unbelievable. I don't care if you're nine years old or ninety. There are just some things that everybody ought to know. Like, there are fifty states. George Washington was the first president. And the Beatles were the greatest rock group ever.

"Hey, I'm reading this book I got out of the library," Birdie told me. "*Golf for Morons*. I'm going to be a great coach."

I've always felt uneasy about people teaching me

things and doing favors for me. I like to do things and learn things on my own. I taught myself how to play guitar. I taught myself how to ride a bike. I taught myself lots of things. I get satisfaction out of learning on my own. But sometimes I have to rely on other people.

"I'll make a deal with you," I told Birdie. "You can be my coach on one condition."

"What's that?"

"You have to let me coach *you* at something."

"There's nothing I want to learn," she said.

"Well, I'm sorry," I told her. "Then you can't be my golf coach."

"What could you teach me, anyway?" asked Birdie.

"I could teach you how to play guitar."

"Oh, I could never do that. It's too hard."

"Don't be ridiculous," I said, putting the Yamaha in her hands. "All you need to know is where to put your fingers. Look, I'm going to show you how to make a D chord."

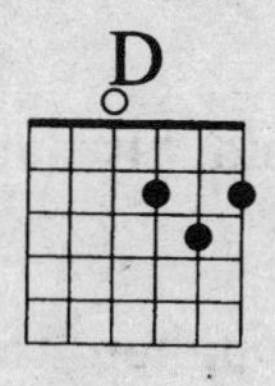

We sat down and I put Birdie's left hand on the neck of the guitar and slid it up to the second fret.

"You only need to touch the bottom three strings," I explained. "Put your index finger here, on the second fret of the third string from the bottom."

"Like this?" she asked.

"Yeah. Now put your middle finger *here*, on the second fret of the first string. Good. Now, put your ring finger *here*, on the third fret of the second string."

I pushed her fingers where they needed to be until they formed the little triangle that is the D chord.

"Good. Now, press down on the strings with all three fingers and strum with your other hand."

She did, and it sounded horrible. It was worse than fingernails on a chalkboard.

"Good," I lied. "This time, curl your fingers a little higher so they only touch the strings they're supposed to touch. If you touch the other strings, they'll buzz. And when you strum, only hit the bottom four strings. I forgot to tell you that."

She played the chord again, and it sounded a little better.

"Ouch!" Birdie said. "It hurts my fingers to press down on the strings."

"You need to toughen them up," I explained. "Build up calluses. If you practice every day, soon your fingers won't hurt anymore."

"But I don't even have a guitar."

"You can borrow my Yamaha," I said. "After all, you fixed it. I have another guitar inside."

Birdie played the D chord a few more times, until it sounded vaguely D-like.

"How many chords are there?" she asked.

"About a million," I replied.

"I know I'm not supposed to ask," Birdie said, "but I really want to know what it's like to be blind."

"It's a lot like being sighted," I replied, "except for the seeing part."

"No, really!" she said, giggling.

"You want to know what it's like to be blind?" I asked.

"Yeah."

"Come with me."

Birdie put the Yamaha down and I took her hand.

"Where are we going?" she asked.

"You'll see . . . I mean, find out."

My dad was out grocery shopping. I led Birdie up the back steps to my house.

"Should I close my eyes?" Birdie asked.

"No need."

We went inside and I opened the door to the basement. After we were both through it, I closed the door behind us.

"It's pitch-dark in here!" Birdie said.

"That's the idea."

Our basement isn't a "finished" basement like Birdie's. We don't hang out and watch TV or anything down there. We use it for storage. It's pretty much filled with junk. Lawn tools, laundry stuff, and who knows what. It's a mess, and I don't go down there very often. There's a light switch somewhere on a wall, but I never bothered to find out where it was. What use do I have for light switches?

"Be careful," I warned Birdie. "The ceiling is low in some places."

"What if I hit my head?" she asked.

"It will hurt," I replied.

I led her around the basement slowly, because I could tell she was nervous being in this dark room filled with sharp objects. Her hand was sweating. Every so often I would stop and put her hand on something.

"What's this?" I'd ask.

"It's . . . a rake!" she said.

"And what's in this box?"

"It's . . . I don't know," she said. "Something cold."

"Loose bathroom tiles," I told her. "Now let go of my hand."

"No!" she said. "I'm scared."

"Come on!" I said. "You think blind kids get led around by the hand all day? If you're going to be blind, you've got to learn how to be independent."

"Okay . . ." she said hesitantly.

We separated, and I let Birdie wander around for a while. She was terrified, but she didn't panic.

"There's a wheelbarrow over here," she reported, "and some kind of a weirdly shaped garbage can."

"That's an old toilet bowl," I said. "But you had the right idea."

Birdie poked around a while longer, and then I decided that was enough blindness for her for one day. I didn't want her to bump into something or fall down and get hurt.

"We should go back upstairs," I told her.

"Hey, what's this?" she asked.

"What's what?"

"There are golf clubs down here," she said.

"That's impossible," I said. "It must be something else."

"Go ahead," Birdie said, "feel them."

I made my way over to where she was and put my

hands where hers were. She was right! It was a bag with a bunch of golf clubs in it. Some were woods and some were irons.

"This is strange," I said.

"Look, there's another bag underneath here!" Birdie said.

I had been down in the basement plenty of times, but I'd never come across any golf clubs. The second bag was also filled with clubs. I could tell that the second set of clubs was smaller. When I put my hand on a few of the clubheads, I discovered something else. They were for a left-handed player. I took one of the clubs out to get a feel for it. It was about the right size for me.

"This is strange," I repeated.

"What's so strange about it?" Birdie asked.

"My dad doesn't play golf," I said, "and he's right-handed."

CHAPTER 10

Double Birdie

THE FIRST THING I did when my dad got home was ask him about the golf clubs I found. I always thought he *hated* golf. Why would he have two sets of golf clubs hidden down in the basement? And why would one set be for a lefty?

"I found 'em in the trash," he said. "I guess some guys got frustrated after a bad round and decided to call it quits. It happens all the time. But you know me. I'm a treasure hunter. Nothing is garbage. I figured I can sell 'em one day. I just never got around to it."

I'm hoping he never will. The first chance I got, I

brought the set of lefty clubs out to the backyard and cleaned them off. They seemed to be in pretty good shape. There were three woods, five irons, a pitching wedge, and a putter. I took a couple of swings with the driver. The clubhead skimmed the grass. The clubs were the right length for me. They felt good.

"Hey, duffer!" somebody shouted. It was Birdie's voice.

"What's a duffer?" I asked.

"A bad golfer," she replied. "I'm halfway through *Golf for Morons*. I'm practically an expert."

Birdie said the clubs looked like they were brand new. There was hardly a scratch on them. She said we should go to a golf course and try them out.

One problem: how could we get to a golf course? There was no way I could carry both Birdie *and* the bag of golf clubs on my bike at the same time.

"This is ridiculous," I told her. "You're thirteen years old. It's time you learned how to ride a bike."

"I tried when I was little," she said. "It was not a pretty sight."

"You're not little anymore," I told her, "and you sit around the house all day because you can't ride a bike. Let's go."

She didn't put up much of a fight. How could she?

I shamed her into it. If a blind kid could ride a bike, she had no excuse.

We wheeled her mom's mountain bike out of the garage. It was decent. Maybe a little small, but it's not like we were going to be entering her in the Tour de France or anything.

The parking lot at the bank down the street is pretty big. That's where I learned to ride. It's perfect because it has a nice gentle slope, so you can use gravity to get you started instead of having to pedal. I remember that when I learned how to ride, I was afraid to take my feet off the ground and put them on the pedals.

We rolled the bike over to the parking lot. The bank was closed. Birdie said there were just a few cars in the lot, and they were way over on the other side. We rolled the bike to the top of the slope.

"Okay, get on," I ordered her.

"This is scary," she said, putting her leg over the bike while I held it. "What if I fall?"

"It will hurt," I told her. "But you're not going to fall. A turning wheel *wants* to stay upright. The only way you can fall is if the wheel stops turning. So all you have to do is give yourself a nice push at the start and then put your feet on the pedals. Trust me."

“I’m afraid,” she said.

“The only thing you have to fear is fear itself,” I said. “That, and cracking your skull open.”

I gave the bike a push.

“Wait!” she screamed. “I’m not ready!”

Too bad. She was already rolling down the hill.

“Now put your feet up on the pedals!” I shouted. “Start pedaling!”

I listened carefully for a bloodcurdling shriek, crying, or the sound of bones breaking. It didn’t come. I guess she must have started pedaling. Because if she didn’t, she would have crashed when the parking lot leveled off.

“WHEEEEEEE!” Birdie screamed from all the way across the lot.

“KEEP PEDALING!” I hollered. “AND DON’T FORGET TO STEER!”

Of course she could ride a bike! Anybody can ride a bike. It was astonishing to think that Birdie had been too afraid to learn. How much fun had she missed all those years she refused to try? What else was she missing in the real world because she spent all her time in her basement building fake worlds on a table?

“I’M RIDING!” Birdie shouted as she circled

around me. She was as excited as a five-year-old. "LOOK AT ME!"

I wished I could. The more I got to know Birdie, the more I wanted to know about her. How could anyone be so frightened that they never learned how to ride a bike? And why didn't she have other friends to hang out with besides me?

There was another question on my mind, too. Were we just friends, or were we more than friends? I never had a "girlfriend." Was Birdie my first girlfriend?

She quickly got the hang of leaning into the turns and using the brakes to slow down. After a few laps around the parking lot, Birdie was riding like she had been doing it all her life. We went back to my house to get my bike and the golf clubs. I stuck my cane in the golf bag and slung the bag over my shoulder.

Now that Birdie could ride, we could go to any of the ten golf courses around Waikoloa. I figured that for her first time out on the bike, we should go to the closest one, Big Island Country Club. It's about a mile away, down Mamalahoa Road.

Before we got on the road, I taught Birdie the system I use for directions. It's based on the face of a clock. If something is directly to my right, I say it's at three o'clock. If it's directly to my left, it's at nine o'clock. In front of me is twelve o'clock, and behind me is six o'clock. It's an easy way to communicate.

There was hardly any traffic, which was good. I had Birdie ride in front of me, and I told her to keep talking so I'd know where she was, when to turn, slow down, or stop.

"Pothole at one o'clock!" Birdie would yell. "Burger King at eleven o'clock!"

I bumped into her back wheel a few times, but we made it to the golf course without any major collisions. We parked the bikes. I opened up my cane and we went in the clubhouse. Birdie found a guy at a desk to talk to.

"My friend here would like to play a round of golf," she said.

"Are you members?" the guy asked.

"No," I said.

"This is not a public course," he told us. "You have to be a member of the country club to play here."

"Oh, come on," Birdie said. "Have a heart. My friend is blind."

"I'm sorry," said the guy. "Members only."

"How much does it cost to be a member?" Birdie asked.

"Fifty thousand dollars."

"Okaaaaay . . ."

We walked back out to the parking lot. Birdie said the guy was a snooty jerk for not letting us play, what with me being blind and all.

"I've been meaning to talk to you about that," I told her. "Could you maybe not mention to everybody that I'm blind?"

"Sure. Sorry. Is that offensive?"

I explained to Birdie that I didn't want people doing special favors for me just because I couldn't see. I wanted to be treated like anyone else. She said she understood.

"That guy was still a snooty jerk," she said. "Fifty thousand dollars! I wouldn't want to be a member of this dump anyway."

"Hey, you know what we should do?" I said.

"What?"

"Let's sneak on the course!" I whispered.

"Are you serious?" Birdie said. "Isn't that illegal?"

"It's illegal like jaywalking is illegal. Everybody does it. Come on, let's go."

"What if we get caught?" she asked.

"They'll probably pull our fingernails out," I said. "Or there's always the ancient Chinese water torture."

We walked around to the other side of the clubhouse, looking for a good place to sneak on. There was a bunch of golfers near the first tee, so we circled around and cut across the grass on the other side. I didn't need to use my cane because Birdie said there was nothing but grass as far as she could see.

"Act like you belong," I told her. "Pretend you have a lot of money and a yacht and stuff."

"All the other golfers are riding around in those cute little carts," she said.

"That's probably another ten thousand bucks."

We walked a long way across a few fairways and finally came to the tee area of the eighth hole. Birdie said there was a wooden sign that said the distance was 152 yards from the tee to the hole and it was a par three. I explained to Birdie that meant a golfer should be able to hit the ball into the hole in three strokes.

"Four strokes would be a bogey and two would be a birdie, right?" she asked.

"Very good!" I said, impressed.

"I've been studying *Golf for Morons*."

"Anybody around?" I asked.

"Just us," she said.

"Let's play it."

"Okay!" Birdie said.

Before we left my house, I had put some golf balls

and tees in one of the pockets of the golf bag. I took out one of each.

"Which club do you think I should use?" I asked Birdie.

"How should I know?" she asked.

"You're the coach," I reminded her.

"Well, here," she said, handing me a club. "This one looks nice."

I felt the head. It was a wood. There was a number "1" carved in it.

"That's the driver," I told Birdie. "If I hit it well, it will drive the ball about two hundred yards, but the hole is only one hundred fifty-two yards away. Let's try the five iron. That will hit the ball higher in the air, and not so far."

"Oooh, listen to you," Birdie said. "Mr. Golf!"

We switched clubs. I stuck the tee into the grass and put the ball on top of it. Then I stepped back a few yards and took a few practice swings.

"Is the coast still clear?" I asked.

"There's nobody around as far as the eye can see."

"Thanks," I said. "My eye can see about two inches. What does the hole look like?"

"How should I know?" Birdie asked. "It's a

hundred fifty-two yards away. I think we can safely assume it's round."

"I mean, describe the terrain for me."

"Well, there's a lot of grass out there," Birdie reported.

"Duh!" I said. "Anything else I need to know?"

"It's a pretty straight shot," she said. "It goes downhill a little, and there's one of those sand thingies on the right side of the green thingie."

"It's called a sand trap," I told her. "Any trees or bushes between me and the green?"

"Nope," she said. "There is a line of trees all the way over on the left side, though."

"Is there any water I need to worry about?" I asked. "A pond? A stream? I know there's no babbling brook, because I would hear it babbling."

"Nope. No water."

"The wind feels like it's blowing from left to right," I said.

"Yeah," Birdie agreed, "and the flag thingie that's stuck in the hole is blowing that way, too."

"Okay, set me up, coach," I said, walking back toward the ball.

Birdie got down on her hands and knees and positioned the clubhead behind the ball. I kept it there while I moved my body until I was lined up with the ball and comfortable. I got ready to swing.

"Hurry up!" Birdie said. "I think I see one of those golf cart thingies in the distance!"

"Shhhh!" I said. "I'm trying to concentrate! You're supposed to be quiet when somebody's about to hit the ball."

"Just go!"

I brought the club back and took a rip at the ball. It made a nice click on contact. But I couldn't tell if it was a good shot or not.

"It's up in the air," she said.

"That's good."

"It's coming down," she said.

"I should hope so."

"It bounced on the green thingie," she said.

"It's just called the green."

"The ball is rolling," she said, her voice rising a little.

"Rolling where?"

"Toward the flag thingie," she said.

"Really?"

"It might hit the flag!" she said.

"Are you putting me on?!"

"Wait!" she said. "The ball disappeared!"

"What do you mean, it disappeared? GOLF BALLS DON'T DISAPPEAR!" I was shouting now.

"I think it . . . went in the hole!" she said.

"It went in the hole?"

"IT WENT IN THE HOLE!" she screamed.

"That's a hole in one!"

"THAT'S A GOOD THING, RIGHT?" she screamed.

"IT'S INCREDIBLE!" I screamed. "I got a hole in one! I got a hole in one! I got a hole in one!"

"Thanks to my great coaching," Birdie yelled.

Birdie and I were jumping up and down and going crazy.

"Hey, you two!" somebody yelled in the distance. "Are you members here?"

"Uh-oh!"

"Let's get out of here!" I told Birdie.

"What about the ball?" Birdie asked. "It's still in the hole. Don't those things cost, like, three dollars each?"

"Forget about the ball!"

We tore out of there as fast as we could go. We didn't slow down until we were on our bikes and back on the road home.

"I don't know why everybody says golf is so hard to play," Birdie said.

CHAPTER 11
Long-distance Putting

"DID YOU TELL your dad about the hole in one?" Birdie asked when she came over after school the next day.

"No way."

I didn't tell *anybody* about the hole in one. Nobody would have believed me, least of all my dad.

It's all luck anyway, when you think about it. Nobody really *tries* for a hole in one. You just try to hit the ball in the general direction of the hole and hope it lands somewhere close on the green. One in a million times or so, it finds its way in the hole. It doesn't matter if you're blind or if you have 20/20 vision. I knew that I just got lucky on that shot.

Birdie came over because she wanted to play her D chord for me. I went upstairs to get my Martin, and handed it to her. She played the D, and it didn't sound half bad. It sounded good, in fact. She had obviously been practicing.

"There aren't any songs with just D chords, are there?" she asked.

"I don't think so," I said. "Are you ready to learn another chord?"

"Sure!"

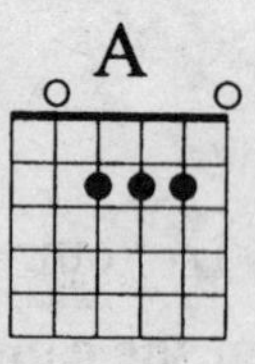

"This time," I said, taking her hand, "I want you to put your first, middle, and ring fingers together and put them *here*, on the second fret of the second, third, and fourth strings. One finger on each string. Got it? Now press hard, and then strum all the strings except the top one, the thickest one."

"Like this?" Birdie said as she played the chord.

It sounded horrible, but it always sounds horrible the first time you play a chord. It takes a while for your fingers to get used to the position, and to make sure you're not touching any of the other strings.

"Good," I said. "That's an A chord."

Birdie played the A again, and already it sounded better. She strummed it a few more times and promised to practice at home.

"So when are we gonna play golf again, coach?" I asked.

"I just finished *Golf for Morons*," Birdie said. "Did you know that about half the strokes a golfer takes are putts? You're not going to get a hole in one every time. We're going to need to work on your putting."

"I don't think we should sneak on the golf course again," I said. "That guy sounded pretty mad when he chased us away."

"I have an idea," Birdie replied. "Let's go miniature golfing!"

It made a lot of sense. Miniature golf is *all* putting. What better way could there be to practice putting than by going miniature golfing? Plus, it was cheaper.

Jungle River Mini Golf is one of the coolest mini golf courses in the world. They have all the usual windmills and loops and stuff. But the whole place is a simulated tropical rain forest. They've got a fog machine, giant waterfalls, a tar pit with animal bones, a giant T. rex, monkeypod trees, banana plants, and jungle sound effects. They really went all out when they built the place. The visual stuff is wasted on me, of course, but people come from all over to play at Jungle River.

I grabbed some money and my cell phone and we got out our bikes. It was a longer ride, and this time we had to cross some busy intersections. Birdie was already riding like a pro, but even so we had a few near misses. When we reached Auhili Loop, some guy in an SUV made a right turn on a red light in front of us, almost hitting her front wheel.

"Jerk!" she screamed at the guy.

"What are you, blind?" I added for the heck of it. "Who taught you how to drive, Ray Charles?"

Finally, we reached Jungle River. I paid six dollars and the lady behind the counter gave me a putter and a golf ball. Birdie led me to the first hole. You had to hit the ball into the mouth of a giant elephant, and then it dropped out the elephant's butt about ten feet from the hole.

It was fairly easy getting the ball into the elephant's mouth, which was about five feet wide. I wasn't nearly as good at making the ten-foot putt.

We tried it over and over again. Birdie would put

the head of the putter behind the ball. Then she would run over to the hole and tell me how hard to hit it, which way the green sloped, and so on. I would use the sound of her voice to give me a clue where the hole was. Even so, I missed the putt five times in a row. I just wasn't good at putting.

"I have an idea," Birdie said. "Give me your cell phone."

"You need to call home?" I asked, handing her my phone.

"No, silly," she said. "Just hold on a sec, and be ready to putt."

I got into position, and suddenly I heard the sound of my cell phone ringing.

"That's probably my dad calling," I said.

"No it's not," Birdie said. "It's *me* calling your phone with my phone. I put yours in the hole so you'd know where it was."

Smart! The phone rang a second time. Birdie was right. I could tell exactly where the hole was. After the third ring, I brought back my putter and rolled the ball toward the sound of the tones. The ball rattled into the cup.

"Right down the middle!" Birdie exclaimed. "Like a heat-seeking missile!"

"Isn't that illegal?" I asked.

"Hey, jaywalking is illegal," she said. "What are they going to do, pull your fingernails out? Give you the Chinese water torture because you put your cell phone in the hole?"

We played all eighteen holes, and I was getting pretty good. Thanks to the cell phone trick, any putt within four feet was just about a sure thing. At ten feet, I'd get it in about half the time. That's not bad, even for a good golfer.

As we walked back to our bikes, Birdie told me she'd been thinking it over, and she decided that golf was the only sport she really liked.

"In all the other sports," she explained, "you want to have the *most*. The most runs, most touchdowns, points, goals, or whatever. But in golf, you want to have the *least*. The player who has the *fewest* strokes is the winner. There's something simple and beautiful about that."

I'd never thought of it that way.

I was really starting to like this girl.

CHAPTER 12

Bad Day for Golf

"SO THIS BLIND GUY walks into a store with his Seeing Eye dog . . .

It was Hunter. We were in homeroom and I could hear him from about twenty feet away. He wasn't making any effort to keep his voice down. I knew what he was up to. He was trying to get to me.

". . . and all of a sudden, he grabs the leash and starts swinging the dog around and around over his head," Hunter said. "The store manager comes running over and yells, 'Are you crazy? What are you doing?' And the blind guy says, 'Oh, I'm just looking around.'"

Everybody cracked up. I did too. It was a funny joke, I had to admit. I'd heard it a million times. I tell that joke myself.

Even if I was offended, I wouldn't have let Hunter know. That's exactly what he wanted.

But ever since the day I beat him at the driving range, Hunter was doing his best to make my life miserable. Telling blind jokes, moving my chair a few inches to one side so I'd bump into it, little things like that.

One morning I found a rubber snake in my desk. I'm sure Hunter put it there. He probably thought I would touch it and freak out. I knew instantly that it was fake. Hunter got really mad when I put the snake around my neck and started petting it.

School wasn't much fun, but I was really enjoying the time I spent with Birdie. She was interesting to talk to, and fun to be with. We held hands a lot, and I liked that. I'd never held hands with a girl before. I wasn't sure if she was holding my hand because she liked me or because I was blind. For all I knew, maybe she held *everybody's* hand. Still, it was nice.

I wanted to tell Birdie I liked her, but I was afraid to say it. What if she just wanted to be friends? If I told her I liked her, it might spoil our friendship.

"Hey, I just got my allowance," Birdie said one

day after school. "What do you say we go shoot a round?"

My dad didn't want me playing golf. But I'm not a baby. He couldn't stop me. It's a free country. He never said, "I forbid you to play golf." All the same, I didn't particularly want him to know I was at a golf course. I wrote a note and left it on the kitchen table.

WENT OUT TO GET SHAVE ICE

WITH BIRDIE.

Birdie and I rode our bikes over to Lua Kula, a public course a little more than a mile away. Birdie had been on their Web site, and it said that anyone under fifteen pays whatever their age is. So if you're thirteen years old, you can play a round for thirteen dollars. Nice deal.

Birdie wanted to pay for me, but I insisted that we split it. After we paid the money, she got a scorecard and led me out to the first tee.

"Okay," she said, putting down the bag of clubs. "This is a short par four, two hundred eighty yards. It bends a little to the right, and there's a cluster of palm trees in the middle of the fairway, about one hundred eighty yards away. So you'll want to hit your tee shot to the left, or you could be stuck behind them. There's a little stream cutting across at one hundred fifty yards, but I'm pretty sure you'll hit it past that. Here's your driver."

Birdie really *had* studied that book. She sounded like she knew what she was talking about. By now, she probably knew more about golf than I did.

I took a ball out of the bag and teed it up. Birdie put the clubhead behind the ball.

"Okay," she said, "give it a ride."

I brought back the club and whaled it. Then I waited for Birdie's report.

"Not bad," she said after the ball had stopped rolling. "We're a little to the left, which is good, about one hundred seventy-five yards away. We didn't hit the trees. I think we're in good shape."

Birdie picked up my bag, and we went to look for the ball. The grass felt good under my feet. Usually when I go walking, I try to stay on the concrete. If I feel sidewalk beneath me, I know I won't get lost. I walk slowly, so that if I bump into anything, at least it won't be a big collision. But Birdie told me the fairway was grassy and wide, so I didn't have to worry.

After a little searching, she found the ball.

"We're about one hundred yards from the hole," she said. "I suggest we use the nine iron."

"Whatever you say, coach."

Birdie told me there was a sand trap on the right side of the green and a pond on the left, so I should try to avoid them. She lined me up for the shot. I could tell the wind was blowing to the right, so I made a minor adjustment for it.

"Let's see if we can put this one on the green from here," Birdie said. "Then we should be able to two-putt from there to make par."

Easy for *her* to say! I took the shot and it felt pretty good, but I could tell that Birdie wasn't happy by her moans and grunts.

"We're about twenty yards short of the green," she said as we walked toward the hole. "But we can chip it on easily from there."

As we walked toward the green, Birdie gave me the pitching wedge from the bag. This would be our third shot. We found the ball and set up to chip it on the green. Birdie told me to move my legs a little closer together, because the book told her you're supposed to do that for shorter shots.

"How far are we?" I asked.

"The hole is toward the back of the green," she

said. “Less than forty yards, I’d say. Don’t hit it too hard. Nice and easy. Bounce it up there in front of the green and let it roll the rest of the way to the hole.”

I choked up on the club a bit and took a little half swing.

“Oh, yes!” Birdie said. “That is a pretty shot.”

The ball was five feet from the pin. As we walked to the green, Birdie kept telling me what a great chip I had made. If I could sink the putt, I would par the hole. Birdie put her cell phone in the hole and I gave her mine so she could call it.

“The green slopes a little to the right,” she told me. I could feel it, too.

“How much, you think?” I asked.

“A couple of inches, tops,” she said. “Not a lot.”

I tried to get a better feeling for how far five feet was. I’m a little over five feet tall. I lay down on the green with my feet near the ball. I felt around until I could put my hand in the hole and touch the cell phone.

“Get the idea?” Birdie asked.

“Yeah.” I got up and Birdie handed me my putter. She put the head behind the ball and lined me up.

“E.T., phone home,” I said.

Birdie made the call and her cell phone rang. She had one of those musical ring tones. The notes were instantly recognizable. It was "Blackbird."

"Where did you get that?" I asked.

"I downloaded it," she explained. "It's my new favorite song."

I focused on the music and aimed for the sound. The ball rolled for a few seconds, and then I heard it rattle into the cup.

"You drilled it!" Birdie said.

"That's four shots," I said. "Put me down for a par."

Birdie marked it down on the scorecard, and we moved on to the next hole. We made a par on that one, too. We got a bogey on the third hole. Then I messed up the next one pretty badly, taking seven strokes for a par three. But all in all I was hitting the ball well and we were having fun.

Birdie seemed to be getting a little tired. I could tell. We had walked a long way, and a golf bag with ten clubs in it is heavy. I could hear her breathing as she walked. I offered to carry the bag, but Birdie insisted that it was part of her job as my coach.

After the ninth or tenth hole, I began to notice it was getting colder out. I didn't bother mentioning it to Birdie. Sighted people don't usually feel it when the temperature changes a degree or two, but I do.

When it started drizzling, Birdie noticed, of course.

We hadn't brought an umbrella or anything to protect us from the rain. I had just made a six-foot putt for a par on the thirteenth hole. The wind was picking up.

"What does the sky look like?" I asked Birdie. "Do you think we should get inside before the rain really starts coming down?"

"We only have a few more holes," she said. "I don't think it will be too bad."

So we kept playing. We were on the seventeenth hole when very suddenly, the drizzle turned into a downpour. It was like someone in the sky was pouring a gigantic pitcher of water over us.

"I'm getting soaked!" Birdie yelled over the howling wind.

"No kidding!"

A second later there was a flash of lightning. I could see the sky light up. That's how bright it was. It must have been close. A clap of thunder followed a second later. We were in trouble.

"Let's get under a tree and wait it out!" I yelled.

"It's an electrical storm," Birdie yelled back. "Standing under a tree is the *worst* thing you can do! Trees are natural lightning rods! We need to make a run for it!"

I grabbed the bag of clubs from Birdie and slung

it over my shoulder. She took my other hand.

"Which way is the clubhouse from here?" I yelled.

"I don't know," she yelled back. "I can't see a thing."

"That makes two of us!"

Thunder was cracking. We were soaked to the skin. We started running and got about fifty yards when Birdie suddenly stopped. She was doubled over, gasping, panting, and coughing.

"Are you okay?" I asked.

"I think . . . I'm having . . . an attack." She could barely get out the words.

"A heart attack?" I asked, alarmed.

"No, an . . . asthma attack," she replied.

"You never told me you had asthma," I said.

"Well, I'm telling . . . you now. I need . . . to take . . . my medicine."

Birdie dug around in her pockets until she found a plastic thing that she sticks in her mouth, and it delivers medicine when she inhales. She sniffed it a few times and then put it away. She was still doubled over.

"Climb on my back!" I shouted, bending down for her. I was already carrying the bag full of clubs, and once Birdie got on me, I was really struggling to walk. But I had to do it. She could barely breathe. I just kept moving. I didn't even know where we were going.

The rain had let up a bit, but it was still pounding all around us. Birdie finally spotted the clubhouse and we struggled to get there. My feet squished inside my sneakers. I was gasping for breath myself.

"Can you make it?" she wheezed.

"I won't need to take a shower tonight," I said.

Finally we reached the porch of the clubhouse. We were drenched, but otherwise okay. Birdie was starting to breathe normally again. I don't know if you can die from an asthma attack, but for a minute there, I was afraid it was all over for Birdie.

We collapsed in a swinging chair on the porch. Rain rapped against the roof. Birdie told me she'd gotten asthma when she was about three years old, around the same time I started losing my vision. What happens with asthma is that the breathing tubes in your lungs get narrow and clogged with mucus as a response to certain "triggers" like stress, cold air, or exercise. Even laughing or crying can set off an attack. Birdie has to take a lot of medicine every day.

"How come you never told me you had asthma?" I asked her.

"It's no big thing."

It seemed like a big thing to me. But I could understand why she never told me. To sighted people, blindness seems like a *really* big thing. She would feel like it would be selfish to bring up her disability when mine was so much more severe, in her eyes.

But I've been blind just about as long as I can remember. I hardly even think of blindness as a disability. I sure wouldn't want to have asthma. I think I would worry all the time about when my next attack would come. At least blindness is something you can count on every day. It's predictable.

My cell phone rang in my pocket. That was a relief. I was afraid the rain had ruined it.

"Where *are* you?"

It was my dad, and I could tell he was mad. He said he'd been trying to reach me, but he kept getting busy signals. I didn't tell him we had been using the cell phone to help me with my putting. I told him where we were, and he said he'd be over as soon as he could get there.

The rain was down to a drizzle. While we were waiting for my dad to come pick us up, we went inside the clubhouse to get warm.

"Whatsa matter," a guy said, "'fraid of a little rain? Hey, just kiddin'. Take these before ya drip all over the floor."

He handed us towels, and we thanked him. He

told us his name was Mr. Ho'okena, and he was the tournament manager of the golf club. He was happy about the rain, because it would be good for the grass.

"So how'd ya do?" he asked.

Our scorecard was soaked, but Birdie was able to add up the score anyway.

"We shot an eighty-two," she said.

"For nine holes?" Mr. Ho'okena asked.

"No, we played eighteen," I said. "Or seventeen, until the rain made us stop."

"Ya shot an eighty-two for seventeen holes?" he said, as if he didn't believe us.

"And he's blind," Birdie said. "I'm just his coach."

"Well, ya don't have to see it to tee it," Mr. Ho'okena said. "Did ya take many mulligans?"

"What's a mulligan?" I asked.

"Ya know, a do-over."

"You can do that?" I asked. It hadn't even occurred to me to take a bad shot over.

"Everybody does," Mr. Ho'okena said. "Y'know, there's a big tournament for kids comin' up in a coupla weeks. You two oughta enter."

"What's the prize?" Birdie asked.

"A million bucks."

"Get outta here," I said.

"I mean it," Mr. Ho'okena insisted. "The guy who built this course back in the 1920s, Angus Killick, said in his will that every year they should hold a tournament for kids and give one young golfer a million smackers."

"Why would he do that?" Birdie asked.

"Old man Killick was a zillionaire. A million here and a million there was chump change for him. He was nuts, too. So every year we hold the Angus Killick Memorial Golf Tournament. I'm tellin' ya, you could win."

"Oh, we're just beginners," I said.

"If ya can shoot eighty-two for seventeen holes, y'ain't no beginner," Mr. Ho'okena said. "Say, what's your name, son?"

"Ed Bogard."

"Bogard . . . with a D?" Mr. Ho'okena asked. "Hmm, there used to be a guy around here named Bill Bogard. Haven't seen him in years."

"That's my dad's name."

"Bill Bogard is your dad?" he said, like my dad was a celebrity. "You're kidding me."

"No," I insisted. "He's a golf-ball diver."

"He became a diver?" Mr. Ho'okena chuckled. "About ten, fifteen years back, Bill was one of the best players on the Big Island. He coulda made the pro tour."

"What?" I said. "My dad never told me he was a golfer. He always acted like he hated anything to do with golf."

"Why do you think he stopped playing?" Birdie asked.

"Can't say I know," Mr. Ho'okena said. "I just never saw him on the course anymore."

A horn honked outside, and I recognized the sound of my dad's Chevy Silverado. Birdie and I said good-bye to Mr. Ho'okena and ran outside. The rain had just about stopped. Dad was loading our bikes and the clubs into the back of the truck.

"You, sir," Dad said to me, "are grounded!"

CHAPTER 13

Good Lies, Bad Lies

"DO YOU REALIZE you two could have been killed?!"

Dad was shouting at us as Birdie and I climbed inside the truck.

"Lightning and golf are not a good combination!" he continued. "I kept trying to call you! Who were you talking to? Why do you think I gave you the cell phone? It was for emergencies like this. Don't EVER go out on a golf course in the rain!"

Dad didn't want answers to his questions. He just wanted to vent. I had never seen him so upset.

"It was my fault, Mr. Bogard," Birdie said quietly. "We had just a few more holes to play when the rain came."

"Stop it, Birdie," I told her. "It was my fault. I'm sorry, Dad. I won't do it again."

"I was worried sick," Dad said, a little softer, "and *your* parents are probably going out of their minds by now."

"My parents couldn't care less," Birdie said.

As we pulled into our driveway and Dad cut off the engine, a car pulled into Birdie's driveway right next to ours. Dad rolled down the window on the passenger side.

"Oh, no," Birdie groaned.

"I'm Bob Andrews," a guy said cheerfully. He grabbed my hand and pumped it.

"And I'm Shelley."

Birdie's parents! I had been starting to think that Birdie didn't even *have* parents. They were never around.

"Nice to finally meet you," my dad said. "I'm Bill Bogard."

"We just had the most incredible experience!" Birdie's mother gushed. "We went birding in the thunderstorm!"

"The woods were lit up like the Fourth of July!" Birdie's dad said. "We saw a Japanese white-eye, and a honeycreeper, and a Hawaiian hoary bat—"

"I saw two apapanes and an amakihi," Birdie's mom interrupted, "and an iiwi!"

"That was no iiwi," her dad said.

"It was too an iiwi," her mom said. "I could tell by the tail."

"I don't think so," her dad said.

"Anyway," they both agreed, "it was awesome!"

"That's great," Birdie said, without much enthusiasm. Then she whispered in my ear, "My parents are freaks!"

I couldn't believe it. Birdie's mom and dad didn't say a word about where we had been, what we had been doing, or why Birdie was soaking wet. All they cared about were which birds they saw during the storm.

Birdie opened the car door. She apologized again to my dad and said good night.

I thought meeting Birdie's weird parents might make Dad forget about what happened on the golf course, but nothing doing.

"Why did you lie to me?" he asked as soon as Birdie and her parents went inside their house. "I went looking for you at every shave-ice joint on the Kohala Coast."

"Why did you lie to *me*?" I asked quietly.

"Lie about what?"

"The golf clubs down in the basement," I said.

Dad stopped, and it was like all the air went out of him. He hadn't expected that, I could tell.

The next thing I knew, he was crying. Big, sobbing, juicy crying.

I had only heard my dad cry twice before. We used to have a Labrador retriever puppy named Rumpelstiltskin, who got hit by a car one day. Dad cried when it happened, and he cried again when we buried Rumpelstiltskin in the backyard.

"Why didn't you tell me you used to be a great golfer?" I asked, putting my arm around him.

"Who told you?" he asked. He was blowing his nose in a handkerchief.

"The tournament manager over at Lua Kula," I said. "Mr. Ho'okena."

Dad sighed.

"I quit golf," he said.

"Why?" I asked.

Dad took a long time before answering.

"Your mom was quite a golfer," he finally told me.

"She was better than me. I'd read about her in the paper before I ever met her. But she stopped playing when you were born."

"Because she had to take care of me?"

"Yeah. She never wanted to go out after you were born. She didn't want to leave you with a babysitter. She couldn't bear to put you in child care."

"So why did *you* quit playing?" I asked.

"You were four years old and it was your mom's thirtieth birthday. I bought her a new set of clubs and talked her into getting a sitter for just one afternoon so she and I could shoot a round together. To celebrate her birthday, y'know? Thirty years. That's a big one. And that was the day when—"

He started to cry again. He couldn't finish the sentence.

"She got struck by lightning while she was playing golf?" I asked.

"I vowed that I would never play again," Dad said.

"And you put the clubs down in the basement."

"I'm sorry I lied to you," he said.

We held each other for a while without saying anything.

"Mom was left-handed, then?" I asked. "I didn't know that."

"Yeah. Like you."

"You could have told me all this before now," I said. "I could have handled it."

"I didn't want you to feel like it was your fault," he said.

"Instead you feel like it was *your* fault," I told him.

"It *was* my fault," he said.

Neither of us seemed to want to get out of the truck. I think it was good for him to tell me what happened with Mom. He seemed to relax a little. It was like a weight had been lifted off his shoulders.

I was just sitting there, thinking about what he'd told me. It was my dad who finally broke the silence.

"You know what I've been thinking about ever since I read that note you left me?"

"What?"

"That I want some shave ice."

Dad turned the key, and the engine roared to life again. There's a place called Lappert's that makes the best shave ice in Hawai'i. Maybe the best in the world. Along the way over there, Dad told me that when I was little and would take a nap, he and my mom would put me in the backseat and drive over to Lappert's for shave ice.

Dad ordered a lilikoi with sweet adzuki beans at the bottom. I got coconut. We climbed back into the truck to enjoy our shave ices.

"Hey, can I ask you a personal question?" Dad asked between spoonfuls.

"Shoot."

"You sure hang out with that girl Birdie a lot. Do you like her?"

I was a little embarrassed. I didn't want to come out and tell him—or *anybody*—how I felt about Birdie. But I'm sure it was obvious. He probably saw me blushing.

"Yeah, I like her."

"Are you two . . . going out?"

"I really don't know, Dad."

CHAPTER 14

A Million Songs

AS IT TURNED out, Dad couldn't bring himself to ground me for more than a day. But Birdie didn't know that. She felt really bad that I was stuck in the house, and she came over after school to keep me company. She brought along my Yamaha and asked me to play "Blackbird" for her again.

"Have you been practicing your chords?" I asked her when I finished the song.

She showed me her A and D chords, and they were really good. No buzzing at all, and she even remembered not to hit the top string when she strummed.

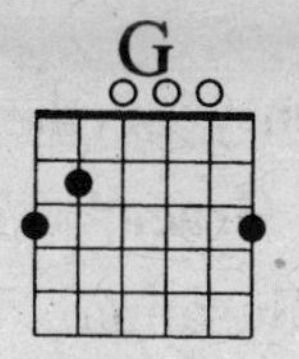

"I think you're ready for your next chord," I said, handing her the guitar. "Here, take your first finger and put it on the second fret of the fifth string. Like this. Good. Now take your middle finger and put it on the third fret of the sixth string. Right. Finally, take your ring finger and put it here, on the third fret of the first string. Now this time, strum *all* the strings."

"Like this?" Birdie asked, playing the chord.

"Curl your fingers higher," I instructed.

"It's pretty," Birdie said, strumming the chord again. "What's it called?"

"G," I told her.

"So now I know three chords," Birdie said, playing each one. "D, A, and G."

"Remember I told you there were a million chords?" I said. "Well, there are. But now that you know three of them, you can play about a million songs."

"No way!" Birdie exclaimed.

"For real," I insisted. "Lots of songs have just three chords."

"Name one," Birdie challenged me.

"I can name plenty of them," I said. "'Happy Birthday,' 'Amazing Grace,' 'When the Saints Go Marching In,' 'Oh Susanna.' Here, let me show you."

Birdie handed back the Yamaha and I played for her. . . .

D G
Oh, give me a home where the buffalo roam

D A
Where the deer and the antelope play.

D G
Where seldom is heard a discouraging word

D A D
And the skies are not cloudy all day.

D A D
Home, home on the range

D A
Where the deer and the antelope play

D G
Where seldom is heard a discouraging word

D A D
And the skies are not cloudy all day.

After the first few words, Birdie joined in. I stopped singing when she started, because her voice is so much better than mine. She sings beautifully.

"See?" I said. "Just three chords in the whole song. D, A, and G."

I gave her the Yamaha and she played "Home on the Range." It was slow, and she messed up a few times on the chord changes, but she played it. It was her first song. I knew a smile was spreading across Birdie's face as she played. I could hear it in her voice. It was like when she rode a bicycle for the first time.

She played "Home on the Range" again, and then I showed her how to use the exact same three chords to play "Blowin' in the Wind." Amazingly, she had never heard it before. How could anyone not know "Blowin' in the Wind"?

I went upstairs to get my Martin so we could play together. I taught her some other three-chord songs: "Wild Thing," "Love Me Do," and "I Shot the Sheriff."

"I can play!" she exclaimed.

By the time we finished "Roll Over Beethoven," Birdie's fingers were hurting and she had to stop.

"Hey," she said. "I've been thinking about that tournament."

"What tournament?"

"Remember?" she said. "That guy at Lua Kula said they have a tournament for kids. The winner gets a million dollars. We could win it, you know."

"I don't think so."

"How do you know?" Birdie asked. "We've got as good a chance as anyone.

"I don't want to enter," I said.

"Why not?"

"I don't want all those people staring at me," I admitted.

Birdie giggled.

"What difference does it make if people stare at you?" she asked. "You can't see them."

If anybody else had said that, I probably would have been offended. But Birdie was Birdie. I couldn't imagine myself getting angry with her. But I did throw a pillow at her.

The screen door slammed, so I knew the mailman had come. I went to the front door and picked up the mail. It's usually just a bunch of catalogs and junk, so I dropped it on the table for my dad.

"There's a letter on top addressed to you," Birdie told me.

"From who?"

"The Lua Kula golf course," she said.

"What do *they* want?"

Birdie opened the envelope and read it out loud. . . .

You are invited by special request
to participate in the 5th annual
Angus Killick Memorial Golf Tournament.
When our founder, Mr. Killick, passed away
in 2000, he instructed that one million dollars from

his estate be set aside each year

to promote youth golf.

I didn't need to hear the rest. Maybe I *could* be angry with Birdie after all.

"Why did you do that?" I demanded.

"Do what?" she asked.

"You signed us up for that tournament!" I accused her.

"I did not!" she replied. "Maybe it was your dad."

"Are you kidding me?"

"Look at you," Birdie said. "You're all upset over nothing. You're sweating. You should play in that tournament. You'll be great."

"I'm not playing!"

CHAPTER 15

The Truth

SATURDAY MORNING. Dad was out delivering the golf balls he'd scooped up all week. I was hanging around listening to some CDs I'd burned.

The doorbell rang. I don't open the door to strangers, because you never know what kind of psycho might be on the prowl.

"Who is it?" I hollered.

"It's me," Birdie yelled. "I need a drink, big-time!"

There was panic in her voice. I could hear her panting.

"Don't be mad at me," she said when I opened the

door. “I didn’t sign you up for that tournament. Cross my heart.”

“Are you having another asthma attack?” I asked, alarmed.

“No,” she said. “I walked over here blindfolded.”

I touched her face and felt the cloth in front of her eyes.

“You still want to know what it’s like to be blind, right?” I asked.

“I almost got killed!” Birdie replied.

Sighted people always think that if they just put on a blindfold, they’ll be able to understand what it’s like to be blind. But as long as you know you can take that blindfold off whenever you want, you’ll *never* know what it’s like to be blind.

Birdie’s house is right next door, but she told me that on the way over, she tripped on the rocks that separate our driveways, crashed into an empty garbage can, and nearly impaled herself on the railing leading up to my front steps. I walk all over the place, and I never think about it twice. But for Birdie to walk next door without seeing, it was like Neil Armstrong taking his first steps on the moon.

“It took me about a half an hour,” she said. “I’m so thirsty.”

"You should use a cane," I told her. "Come on, I'll get you a soda."

"Hold my hand," she pleaded.

"Oh, no, that would be too easy," I said. "Follow the sound of my voice."

Our kitchen is about fifty feet from the front door, but it was an adventure for Birdie. I tried to talk her through it, but she still bumped into every chair and table in the living room. She was grunting and cursing and complaining every time she rammed into something.

"You can do it," I said, encouraging her. "We're almost in the kitchen!"

"Ow! I just smashed my head against something!"

"That's the door frame," I said. "Put your hand in front of your face."

Finally, she made it into the kitchen in one piece. I took a couple of sodas out of the refrigerator and gave her one.

"The blind leading the blind," Birdie said, sitting down and taking a long gulp. "What's this, Sprite? 7UP?"

"You tell me."

"Sprite," she guessed.

"Nice try," I said. "It's Mountain Dew."

"Tastes like Sprite."

"You're not going to walk around blindfolded all day, are you?" I asked her.

"I don't think I could survive an hour," she said. I heard her taking off the blindfold. "How do you do it?"

"It's not like I have a choice," I told her. "People get used to things."

"Are you still mad?" she asked.

"I guess not."

"Listen," she said. "I think I know who entered you in that tournament."

"Who?"

"Remember that guy we met at Lua Kula after the thunderstorm? He said he was the tournament manager."

I remembered the guy. Mr. Ho'okena. He had told us about the tournament and suggested we enter. I even spelled my name for him. Birdie was right. It had to be him.

I told Birdie I was sorry for yelling at her. She accepted the apology. Her breathing had returned to normal.

"What do you wanna do?" she asked.

"I don't know, what do *you* wanna do?"

We played the "I don't know, what do *you*

wanna do?" game until we got bored of doing *that*.

"Where are your parents?" I asked.

"Out birding, of course," Birdie replied. "They got these new binoculars with a built-in digital camera, and now they can't get enough."

Birdie's folks were *always* birding. I would think that even if I could see, I sure wouldn't want to stare at birds all day. But who knows? Maybe birds are so amazing that it's fun. I hardly remembered what birds looked like.

"Want to go to Hapuna Beach?" I suggested.

"I hate the beach," Birdie said. "You've got to worry about jellyfish, rip currents, stepping on sea urchins, and bluebottles. Do you know that when a cone shell stings you, the venom can be fatal?"

"We could go parasailing," I suggested. "Your feet won't even touch the ground."

Parasails are these hang gliders that get pulled by a boat. It's sort of like waterskiing in the air. I did it with my dad a few times. It's really cool.

"You're not going to get me up on one of those things," Birdie said.

"We could go Jet Skiing," I suggested.

"With all the tiger sharks out there?" Birdie said. "No thanks."

"You know, *that's* why you're bored," I told her. "You don't want to do anything."

It slipped out. I really didn't mean to say it. But it was the truth, and it needed to be said. Maybe I was frustrated with Birdie. Maybe I felt comfortable enough around her to give her a little criticism. I'm not sure. But once I got started, I kept going.

"You didn't think you could ride a bike, and you didn't want to try. You didn't think you could play the guitar, and you didn't want to try. You don't think you're good at anything, and you don't want to try anything new. You never go anywhere, and you don't want to do anything! But how are you ever going to get good unless you try new things? What are you afraid of?"

It was a mistake. I should have stopped way earlier. I never should have gotten started, because I suddenly realized that Birdie was crying. I apologized for shooting off my mouth, but it was too late. What's that expression? The toothpaste was out of the tube. There was no way to put it back.

"You're right," Birdie whimpered. "I'm a horrible person."

"I didn't say that!" I insisted. Now she really had me frustrated. "You're twisting things around. It's almost like you want a reason to be down on yourself."

"You're right," she said softly. "I'm a—I don't know what I am."

I sat down on the couch with her and held her.

"When I was in second grade," she said softly, "I was a spelling geek."

"A spelling geek?"

"I could spell anything," she said. "I would memorize the dictionary. I spent hours practicing spelling."

"Why?" I asked.

"I was good at it," she said. "So my parents started entering me in spelling bees. I was the school champion, and then I was county champion, and then I was the best speller in Maine."

"Wow," I said. "You *were* a spelling geek!"

"Kids at school made fun of me so much that I didn't want to go to school," Birdie said. "I wanted to quit, but my parents forced me to go to the National Spelling Bee in Washington."

"How did you do?" I asked.

"I humiliated myself," Birdie said. "I messed up in the first round. When I came home, the kids were brutal to me. I thought I was going to have a nervous breakdown. I wanted to die."

So *that's* why Birdie and her parents moved from Maine. That's why she retreated into this shell she lived in.

"Which word did you mess up on?" I asked.

"Through," she said. "T-H-R-O-U-G-H."

"How did you spell it?" I asked.

"T-H-R-O-U-G-H-T," she said. "I got confused in the middle. I thought it was 'thought.'"

"That's a common mistake," I told her.

"Not at the National Spelling Bee."

I grabbed Birdie by the hand.

"Where are we going?" she asked as I pulled her out the door.

"You'll find out when we get there."

Jet Skis are sort of like motorcycles that ride on water. The throttle is on the right handlebar. When you twist it, the engine roars and you go faster. They are so cool.

We rode our bikes over to Spencer Beach Park, where they rent Jet Skis. This guy George, who is a friend of my dad's, works there, and he said I could come over and Jet Ski anytime for free.

"I'm not getting on one of those monsters," Birdie said as soon as she saw what I had in mind.

"Oh yes you are."

"I'm going to drown."

"No you won't."

"What happens if I fall off?"

"It will hurt."

My friend George said aloha and handed us life jackets. Because Birdie had never done it before, she had to sign some form saying she wouldn't sue even if she was mangled or paralyzed while Jet Skiing.

"I'll sit behind you," Birdie said after George led us to our Jet Ski.

"Maybe you should sit in the front, miss," George suggested. "You're the eyes."

Birdie had a ball Jet Skiing, as I knew she would. Then I took the controls and Birdie went nuts, *screaming* the whole time to turn left, turn right, slow down, and WATCH OUT FOR THAT BOAT! It was an insanely good time.

"Okay, I did it," Birdie said when we got off the Jet Ski. "Now, how about you play in the tournament?"

"We've hardly practiced at all," I said. "Some of those kids are going to be good. They've probably been playing all their lives. We would humiliate ourselves."

"Well!" Birdie said. "I never thought I'd hear *you* say you can't do something. Weren't you the guy who said a blind person could do anything a sighted person could do?"

"Except drive," I said.

"We're *good*, Bogie!" Birdie insisted. "We make a great team. That golf teacher said you have a perfect swing. He said he'd never seen anything like it. We can shoot par most of the time. That book I read said that most golfers are *terrible*. Even golfers who are good are terrible a lot of the time. We've got as good a shot as anybody. Come on, I did this for you. Play in the tournament for me."

She was right. If she could confront her fear, I could confront mine.

"Okay, okay," I sighed. "I'll do it."

And then, Birdie kissed me.

It came out of nowhere! She kissed me! Right on the lips and everything. I didn't even have time to get ready. She just did it without warning. It was nice, I must admit.

"What was that for?" I asked.

"I don't know," Birdie said. "Does there have to be a reason for everything?"

"Does this mean we're . . . going out?" I asked.

"You know what your problem is?" Birdie said to me. "You think too much."

CHAPTER 16
Miniature Golf

I DIDN'T SEE BIRDIE for a few days. She didn't come over, and I didn't make any effort to seek her out. It felt weird. We had kissed each other! Were we boyfriend and girlfriend? Or not? Maybe the whole kissing thing was no big deal to her. It was just spontaneous. Maybe I was blowing the whole thing out of proportion. Maybe she kissed people all the time.

I was starting to regret that I said I'd play in the tournament. Golf was fun, but I didn't want to play in front of a lot of people with all of them staring at me like I was some animal in a zoo. I could still back out. I could change my mind.

The doorbell rang after school and it was Birdie.

"I have something to show you," she said in that mysterious way of hers.

"What is it?"

"You'll see," she said, taking my hand.

"No I won't."

She led me outside, across the driveway, and over to her house. We went down the steps to the basement. I remembered where the air hockey table was, and made sure not to bump into it this time. Birdie led me over to the big table where she had built the scale model of Hawai'i.

"Climb up," Birdie instructed.

"But you already showed me this," I said.

"No I didn't."

I hopped up on the table and felt around. It was different. The islands were gone.

"What happened to Hawai'i?" I asked.

"I got bored with it," Birdie said. "A volcano erupted and wiped it off the face of the earth."

"What is this?" I asked, feeling around.

"Guess."

Birdie was giggling. I moved my hand all over the

table, searching for clues. Most of the surface was soft. It was made out of terry cloth or something. There were no mountains, but a lot of little trees. Or maybe they were bushes. The surface was mostly flat, with some gentle hills and valleys.

Every few feet my fingers brushed against what felt like a toothpick sticking out of the ground. Then I noticed some little round patches where there was sand instead of cloth. I could pick up the sand with my fingers.

"It's a golf course!" I announced.

"Right!" Birdie said. "But not just any golf course. It's Lua Kula."

The detail was just amazing. As I examined the surface some more, my fingers touched tiny little people, and tiny little golf carts. Incredible.

"I thought that if I built a little Lua Kula," Birdie said, "you would be able to visualize it better. That way, when we get out there on the first tee, you'll know what to expect."

She took my hand and guided it over to the other side of the table.

"See, this is the first hole. It has a slight dogleg to the right remember? You've got to watch out for these palm trees right in the middle of the fairway, not too far from the green. There's a pond here and a sand trap here. Feel them? And there's a little stream running across here."

"This is the most amazing thing I've never seen!" I said.

"Very funny," Birdie said.

A thought flashed through my mind. Maybe Birdie was crazy. I've seen movies about people who go nuts. Did you ever see *Close Encounters of the Third Kind*? This guy makes a giant mound of mud in his house to welcome the space aliens. Building a perfect scale model, eighteen-hole golf course on a table down in your basement was exactly the kind of thing a psycho would do. Maybe Birdie was losing her mind.

"You probably think I'm crazy," Birdie said.

"Oh no, not at all," I lied.

After all the trouble Birdie had put into simulating Lua Kula, now I *had* to play in the tournament. There was no backing out.

A drop of sweat slid down my armpit. The reality of having to actually play golf in front of people suddenly sank in. I remembered the time I played guitar in the third-grade play. Halfway through the song I forgot the chords and ran off the stage. Now I would have to play golf with a bunch of people staring at me. I was afraid.

* * *

We went over Birdie's miniature Lua Kula inch by inch. It was interesting how no two holes were exactly alike. I memorized where every tree, brook, sand trap, and water hazard were positioned. There were some par-three holes that were less than one hundred fifty yards, and other holes that were longer than five hundred yards. Those were par five. Birdie had actually gone out on the course and taken pictures with a digital camera so her model would be perfect.

I wasn't sure if I should tell my dad about the tournament. Things had gotten better between us ever since he told me what happened to my mom. But what if I totally messed up and humiliated myself? I didn't want him to see that. I decided not to tell him about the tournament.

Birdie and I agreed that if we were going to compete, we'd better start practicing. We had a week to prepare for the tournament. Every day after school we worked on part of our game. One day we went to a driving range to practice our tee shots. One day we went out to an empty field to work on our short game. One day we went over to Hapuna Beach to practice blasting the ball out of sand traps. One day we went miniature golfing to improve our putting.

The tournament was scheduled for Saturday morning. A couple of days before, I got an e-mail from Mr. Ho'okena, the guy Birdie and I met after the thunderstorm. He said there would be a meeting at Lua Kula on Friday afternoon for all the kids in the tournament. Birdie and I rode our bikes over there.

I didn't take my cane along. When you have a cane, suddenly you're the center of attention. I didn't want all the kids to be pointing at me and whispering to each other about the blind golfing freak. Birdie led me into the clubhouse.

"I want to welcome you all to the Angus Killick Memorial . . ."

I recognized the voice of Mr. Ho'okena.

". . . Most of you had to qualify to be here. Some of you got a special invitation. But now all of you have one thing in common. A fair chance to win a million dollars."

"Yeah!" everybody shouted.

"But there's one thing you need to know," Mr. Ho'okena continued. "*Nobody* is gonna win the cash unless they score below forty-five."

"That's five strokes per hole!" somebody complained.

"Mr. Killick didn't want it to be easy," explained Mr. Ho'okena. "But the rules are pretty simple. You each play nine holes. Whoever has the lowest score will be the winner. Besides the million bucks, you get this nice trophy."

I asked Birdie how big the trophy was.

"Bigger than you," she whispered.

"What happens if there's a tie?" somebody asked.

"If two or more players have the same score after nine holes, we'll have a playoff," Mr. Ho'okena said. "They'll go back to the first tee and start again. As soon as somebody wins a hole, that person wins the tournament. Any other questions? Okay, I'll just say good luck. You should be here tomorrow at ten o'clock sharp to tee off. And if you're late, well, *I'll* be teed off."

Everybody laughed and people started milling around.

"Nine o'clock," Birdie whispered in my ear.

"He said ten o'clock," I replied.

"No, I mean there's a boy at nine o'clock who's staring at you. About twenty feet away."

"A lot of people stare at me," I told her. "What does he look like?"

"He's about our age," Birdie reported. "Tall. Good-looking. I think I've seen him before. He's wearing a Waikoloa School T-shirt. He probably goes to school with you."

"I think I know who he is," I told her.

"Who?"

"Hunter Lynch."

"That jerk from school?" Birdie asked.

"Yeah. I guess he's going to be in the tournament, too."

"We've got to beat that guy," Birdie said.

"I thought you didn't like competition," I reminded her. "Didn't you say the world would be a better place if people didn't compete with one another?"

"That was before you told me what a jerk he was," Birdie said. "He's going *down*."

They were giving out doughnuts and apple juice to everyone in the tournament. Birdie got me a plate. I was standing there munching my doughnut when Mr. Ho'okena came over.

"Hey, Ed Bogard! Nice to see you! I'm glad you decided to come. You just might win that million bucks."

"Thanks for sending me the invitation."

"Invitation?" he said. "I didn't send you an invitation."

"You didn't?" I asked. "Then who did?"

"I did."

It was Hunter's voice.

"*You* signed me up? Why?"

"Two reasons, Bogie," Hunter said. "You've got the best swing I ever saw. You should be in this tournament. You deserve to be here."

"What's the other reason?" I asked.

"I want to beat you."

CHAPTER 17

The Tournament

SATURDAY is a busy day on golf courses. Most people don't go to work, so they have time to play. My dad doesn't dive for golf balls on Saturday. He drives all over the Big Island delivering balls to stores, country clubs, and other clients who ordered them.

"What are your plans today?" Dad asked me before he got in the truck to leave.

"Oh, I don't know," I replied. "Maybe hang out with Birdie."

Well, it wasn't a *complete* lie.

It felt like a nice day when Birdie and I were

riding our bikes out to Lua Kula. Pretty hot, but at least there wasn't too much wind. I don't like wind. It makes it hard to judge where to hit the ball.

All the kids in the tournament were gathering in front of the clubhouse. There were thirty-six of us, so they split us into nine groups of four kids each.

Instead of having us all stand in line for an hour waiting for our turn to tee off, they had what is called a "shotgun start." Everybody starts at the same time, with each foursome at a different hole. So we would all finish our nine holes at the same time too.

Birdie and I were assigned to start at the fourth hole. That's where we met up with the rest of our group. There was this little kid named Bryce, who was only nine years old. There were a pair of twin sisters named Franny and Zooey, who said they had gotten special permission to play as a single player, alternating shots. Then there was this big high school kid named Peter, who said his dad wanted him to play football, but he didn't like football. His dad forced him to take up a sport, so he chose golf because his dad hates golf. He didn't want to be there.

All of them seemed nice enough. I was just relieved that Hunter wasn't in our group. He was in the foursome in front of us. So he started on the third hole.

"How many people are watching?" I asked Birdie after shaking hands with the others.

"Nobody," she said. "We're all alone out here."

"You're lying, right?" I asked.

"Yeah," she said. "Just play your game. Don't worry about how many people are watching."

I hadn't taken a shot yet, and my shirt was already sticking to my back.

The fourth hole was a par four. Peter, Bryce, and I decided to be gentlemanly and let Franny and Zooey go first. Zooey hit a grounder that didn't go anywhere, and Franny thought that was the funniest thing in the world. She took a penalty shot and didn't do much better. Peter sliced a ball off into the trees that somebody might find in the next century. The only one who seemed to have any idea of what to do with a golf club was Bryce, the nine-year-old. He hit his tee shot maybe a hundred yards down the fairway. Not very far, but at least it was straight.

"None of these kids are going to give us any problem," Birdie whispered to me before my tee shot. "Just hit it like you know how to hit it."

I remembered what the fourth hole looked like, thanks to the model Birdie made in her basement. There was a line of trees on the left side and a big boulder right in the middle of the fairway about two hundred yards from the tee. We had already discussed that I would just hit my regular tee shot and hope the ball landed to the left or right of the boulder.

Birdie set me up and I took a rip at it. It was a good shot, about 185 yards, a little left of center. The other kids could hardly believe that a blind kid could hit a golf ball at all, much less hit one as far as I did.

"Awesome shot, dude," Bryce told me.

We marched down the fairway and Birdie had no trouble finding our ball. She suggested we hit the seven iron from there. The rest of the foursome was completely blown away when I hit my second shot and the ball rolled on the green about ten feet from the hole.

It took Franny and Zooey about five shots each to get that far. They laughed hysterically each time they took a swipe at the ball and squibbed it ten feet or dug up a huge chunk of grass. I wondered how they could have possibly qualified for the tournament. They must have received a special invitation like me, because they truly sucked at golf. But at least they were having fun.

Peter hooked or sliced just about every shot. He hit the ball a ton, but he couldn't hit it straight. He got more frustrated with each swing. By the time the rest of us reached the green, he had wandered off, and we never saw him again. I guess he realized he had no chance, gave up, and went home.

Bryce three-putted on the green and took a seven for the hole. That's a triple bogey, but not that bad for a kid his age. Franny and Zooey lost track of how many strokes they had taken, so they each put down a ten on their scorecard.

When it was my turn to putt, Birdie and I pulled out our cell phones. She put hers in the hole and lined me up. We both agreed that the putt looked like a straight shot but the green sloped downhill, so I would have to stroke it gently to make sure the ball wouldn't shoot ten feet past the cup.

"Okay, dial it," I told Birdie.

The others thought it was totally cool when Birdie's phone rang and "Blackbird" started playing from the cup. I stroked the ball gently and waited while it rolled. I knew it was going in before the ball rattled into the hole, because Franny and Zooey were shouting, "Looks good!" and "He's gonna make it!" every inch of the way.

"You got a birdie!" Bryce said, clapping his hands. "Man, you are such a rock star!"

We moved on to the next hole. Franny and Zooey

said they were dropping out because they knew they were terrible, but they were going to stay with us anyway so they could be my cheerleaders.

There was an adult volunteer at each tee, I guess to make sure nobody was cheating. When we got up to the tee area on the fifth hole, Birdie asked the volunteer how "that tall kid" in the group before us did. She meant Hunter, of course.

"I think he got a par," the lady replied.

"Good," Birdie said. "That means we're beating him by a stroke."

I got a par on the fifth hole too, but it wasn't easy. I hit my tee shot into the rough on the right side and had to make a miracle shot with my pitching wedge to recover. But I hit a good chip onto the green and a good putt to save par.

I got a bogey on the next hole, and messed things up for a double bogey on the one after that. But Birdie gave me a little pep talk, and that must have inspired me. I birdied the next two holes.

When we arrived at each new hole, Birdie would ask the volunteer how Hunter was doing. For somebody who told me she didn't like competition, she really wanted to win.

From what we could gather, Hunter was playing

well. He could hit the ball, that was for sure. It was impossible to tell his exact score on each hole, or if he was doing as well as we were, because he was always one hole ahead of us. But we were getting the sense that it was close. One of the volunteers told Birdie that, aside from us and Hunter, the rest of the field was dropping away.

I could actually win this thing, I realized. A million bucks. You could buy a lot of stuff with a million bucks. I could finally get the Fender Stratocaster I had been thinking about for years, and a good amp. I could even set up a little recording studio at home, and still have money left over to pay for college. Maybe get Dad a new truck, too.

Knock it off, I told myself. Focus on the shot, not the payoff.

After the first few holes, I wasn't so nervous anymore. That was good, because with each hole we played, more people were following us around. I guess word was spreading. It was like a traffic accident at the side of the road. Everybody wants to stop and watch the blind kid play golf for a million dollars. People were starting to cheer me on.

Fifty? A hundred people? I couldn't tell. I'm not very good at estimating crowds. But I could hear the cameras clicking, the candy wrappers rustling, and the whispering. People like to root for an underdog, I guess.

We had played five or six holes when Birdie asked me if she could sit down on a bench for a minute and take a rest. It was *hot.* I was sweating myself. I forced her to drink some water. I didn't want her to have another asthma attack.

"Let me carry the bag," I said.

"No way," Birdie insisted. "You need to keep your strength up. We have a shot to win this thing."

I could hear her breathing, and I was relieved when we finished up the last hole. I didn't even care that much what our score was. I just wanted to make sure Birdie was okay.

We made par on the last hole, and Birdie tallied up our scorecard. We finished with a 41, which was three strokes over par. Not bad at all. Even if we didn't win, we beat the forty-five-stroke cutoff.

"You rule, dude," said my little friend Bryce, who finished with a 63.

Because we had started on the fourth hole and finished on the third hole, we had a long walk back to the clubhouse. I could tell that Birdie was really struggling at the end. She put our scorecard in a box with all the others, and we waited for one of the volunteers to add them all up.

"What do you think?" I asked Birdie.

"I think I'm ready to take a nap."

Some of the kids left. I guess they missed the cutoff and knew they weren't going to win, so there was no reason to hang around. After about ten minutes, Mr. Ho'okena came out.

"Congratulations to all of you who participated," he said. "I can tell you this right now. Several of you beat the cutoff of forty-five strokes. *Somebody* is gonna leave here with a check for one million big ones."

There was a roar from the crowd.

"In fact, we have a tie," Mr. Ho'okena continued, "between Mr. Hunter Lynch and Mr. Ed Bogard."

Birdie let out a scream that rattled the windows.

CHAPTER 18

Sudden Death

EVERYBODY gathered around and started clapping me on the back as if I had already won the tournament.

"What happens now?" my little friend Bryce asked.

"Sudden death," said Mr. Ho'okena.

Hunter and I would have to go back to the first hole and play each other one-on-one. If he won the hole, he'd win the tournament. If I won the hole, I'd win the tournament. And if we took the same number of strokes, we'd play the second hole. And the third hole, until one of us beat the other.

"Are you going to be okay?" I asked Birdie. I was concerned because she was panting the same way she had been before her asthma attack.

"I'm fine," she said, grabbing the bag of clubs. "Let's get him."

Franny and Zooey came over to say good-bye. They wanted to stick around and see what would happen, but their mom had come to pick them up.

Suddenly I felt an arm over my shoulder, and I knew who it belonged to.

"Bogie, old boy," Hunter said, "remember that day you outdrove me at the driving range?"

"Yeah," I said. "I remember."

"And remember how you wouldn't let me have a rematch?"

"Yeah."

"Well, it looks like I'm gonna finally get my rematch, after all."

"I guess you are."

"Listen," Hunter said. "I've done some mean stuff to you, man. But you really showed me something today. I gotta respect you. And I want to wish you good luck."

"You too, Hunter."

While Hunter had his arm around me, I heard lots of cameras snapping pictures of us.

Hunter said aloha to Birdie before walking away, but she gave him the silent treatment.

"I still hate him!" she whispered. "He's just trying to psych you out."

Birdie and I went out to the first tee. I took a ball out of my bag.

Mr. Ho'okena announced how happy he was to see so many spectators watching us play. He went over the rules for Hunter and me, then asked if either of us had any questions.

"I do," Hunter said. "If Bogie gets to have a coach with him, I think I should be allowed to have a coach with me, too."

"What do *you* need a coach for?" Mr. Ho'okena asked.

Hunter didn't answer. But I heard him take something out of his golf bag. Then the crowd let out a gasp.

"What's he doing?" I asked Birdie.

"He's putting on a blindfold!" she said.

"Are you kidding me?"

She wasn't. The crowd began to applaud.

"Now, *that's* what I call sportsmanship!" somebody yelled.

"I suppose that under the circumstances," Mr. Ho'okena said, "both players can use a coach to assist them."

The crowd applauded again. Hunter asked Ronnie to come out of the crowd and be his coach.

"Did you know Hunter could play blind?" Birdie whispered in my ear.

"He can't," I replied. "He tried it at the driving range. He missed everything."

"Maybe he *was* hustling you," Birdie said.

"Nobody's gonna say I didn't beat you fair and square, Bogie," Hunter said.

Mr. Ho'okena flipped a coin and I called heads while it was in the air. It was tails. Hunter elected to tee off first.

Birdie and I stepped back to give Hunter room to hit his tee shot. He and Ronnie took a long time talking about the shot and lining up. Finally, the crowd got quiet and I heard the whoosh of his club.

"Did he hit it?" I asked Birdie.

"Oh, yeah," she said, "he hit it."

"How far?"

"I don't know," she said. "It didn't come down yet."

The crowd exploded into whistles and applause.

"How far?" I asked again.

"Let me put it this way," Birdie said. "You're lucky you're blind. You wouldn't want to see how far he hit that ball."

Hunter must have been practicing blindfolded. Somebody in the crowd said his tee shot went more than two hundred yards and it was positioned perfectly. That meant he would have an easy second shot to the green. I had to hit a great tee shot, or it might be all over on the first hole.

I pushed my tee into the grass and put a ball on top of it. There was a cluster of palm trees directly in front of the green, I remembered from Birdie's scale model. I'd have to avoid it.

Birdie set me up. In my head, I told myself not to overswing trying to outdrive Hunter. Nice and easy does it. It's when you try too hard that you mess up.

But my muscles weren't listening. I swung as hard as I could.

It felt good, but the crowd went "oooooh!" and I heard the ball hit something hard. I knew it was bad news.

"Too bad," somebody muttered. "He hooked it."

"What happened?" I asked.

"It bounced off one of the trees," Birdie said.

"So where are we?" I asked.

"It came straight back," she replied. "We're in front of the trees."

Hunter's ball was past the trees, on the left. It wasn't a good situation.

"What do we do now?" I asked Birdie.

"We've got to hope he messes up his next shot," she replied. "Because we need to take two shots to get around the trees. There's no other way past them."

Birdie picked up the golf bag and we started walking up the fairway. I imagined Birdie's model golf course, picturing the first hole in my head.

"Bogie," Birdie said as we walked, "I don't feel so good."

"Are you okay?" I asked. "You're not going to have another asthma attack, are you?"

"No, I . . ."

And that was all she said. I heard the golf bag hit the ground, and then Birdie fall on top of it.

"Birdie!" I shouted.

"The girl fainted!" somebody yelled.

"Call an ambulance!"

Everybody came running over, and in seconds people were crowding around shouting that we should give Birdie air, give her water, elevate her head, and all kinds of other advice. One woman said she was a doctor, and the others let her take over.

"She has asthma," I told the doctor.

"It looks more like heatstroke or heat exhaustion,"

the doctor replied. "We've got to get this girl to the hospital."

Birdie was breathing, but she was out cold. The ambulance arrived in seconds, with the siren blaring. It drove right onto the fairway, and some paramedics loaded Birdie into it.

After the ambulance drove away, a feeling of helplessness came over me. What was going to happen to her? Birdie and I were a team. The only golf I had ever played, I had played with her. I didn't know what to do now. I was just standing there. Suddenly, I felt very alone. Somebody put an arm on my shoulder, but it wasn't Hunter. It was Mr. Ho'okena.

"Under the circumstances," he said, "I recommend that we postpone this playoff until your coach is able to participate."

"I guess I don't have any other choice," I agreed.

"Nothing doing," somebody shouted. "I can coach him."

It was my dad's voice!

"Dad! What are *you* doing here?" I asked him.

"I came to watch you play."

"How did you know about the tournament?" I asked.

"Birdie told me about it," he said. "She said it

would mean a lot to you if I could be here. I've been watching you all day, son. You've got a sweet swing, you know that?"

"It runs in the family."

"You can still win this thing, you know," Dad whispered. "It's not over. But you're gonna need a little help."

"Let's go."

"I suppose we can continue," said Mr. Ho'okena, "unless there are any objections."

"He can have Tiger Woods coach him for all I care," said Hunter.

Dad grabbed the bag and took my elbow as we walked up to my ball.

"Now, listen," he whispered. "First thing you've got to do is put Birdie out of your mind. She's gonna be okay. They'll take good care of her."

"I'll try," I said.

"This Hunter kid is in perfect position," Dad said. "He can reach the green easy from where he is, but you can't. You've got some big old coconut palms staring you in the face. If you chip the ball to the side of the trees and then poke your next shot on the green, you'll lose. Because he can get to the same place with just one shot. It looks like you're finished."

“So what makes you say I can win?” I asked.

“Because you *can,*” Dad said, “but you’re gonna have to be a little creative.”

“What do you mean, creative?” I asked.

“You have to hook the ball around the trees,” he said. “You have to shape the shot.”

“What?” I said. “You mean, curve it on purpose? That’s crazy! It’s tough enough just hitting the ball *straight.*”

“You hooked the ball to get here,” he said. “Sometimes the shot that gets you in trouble will get you out of it, too. You have to hook the ball again if you want a chance to win. Trust me. You can do this. He’s over there celebrating with his friend. You wrap that ball around those trees right now and it’ll devastate him. His morale will be shot.”

“You’re the coach,” I sighed.

“Good boy.”

Dad handed me the nine iron and told me that if I wanted to hook the ball to the right, I would have to put a lot of clockwise spin on it. To do that, I had to “close” my stance. That is, he had me move my left foot back and my right foot forward. I also had to close the clubface, which meant rotating it to the right. Finally, he positioned my feet so I was facing more to the left and the ball was closer to my right foot than normal.

"We're aiming just left of the trees," Dad told me. "Take a full swing and hit *down* on the ball a little."

"All that's going to make the ball curve around the trees?"

"Trust me," Dad said.

"Isn't there a pond to the left of the green?" I asked. "If the ball doesn't hook, it will go in the pond."

"Don't worry," Dad said. "If it goes in the pond, I'll dive in and get it."

"Very funny, Dad."

"If you do what I said, the ball will curve right onto the green."

Birdie wouldn't have known any of this, it occurred to me. You can only learn so much from reading *Golf for Morons*. My dad had a lifetime of experience.

Dad checked the wind by tossing a few blades of grass in the air. He told me the hole was about 120 yards away on the other side of the trees. Then he put the clubhead behind the ball for me.

"Now do it," he instructed me. "Show me your curveball."

I brought back the club and smacked the shot just the way he told me to. I didn't hear the ball rattle off a tree, which was good. I didn't hear it splash into the pond, which was even better. I didn't hear anything for a few seconds. The ball was up in the air.

Finally, after what seemed like an eternity, I heard the roar of the crowd.

"Guess what, son?" Dad said. "You're on the green."

CHAPTER 19

Luck and Gravity

EVERYBODY in the crowd was shocked that I'd even *tried* to hook the ball around the trees. When it rolled onto the green, they went nuts, cheering and screaming like I was a superstar. Everybody was asking me if I'd done it on purpose. Dad told me a pro couldn't have hit the shot any better. My ball was about ten feet from the cup. A million dollars was ten feet away.

"Was that luck or skill?" I asked Dad.

"A little of each," he said with a chuckle. "Now the pressure's on *him*. He messes up this shot, and you win."

We stood there for a long time, waiting for Hunter and Ronnie to plan strategy, choose a club, and set up for Hunter's second shot. I don't know what took *him* so long. *He* didn't have to curve the ball around any trees. He had a straight shot to the green. Less than one hundred yards.

Finally, Hunter hit it and I could tell from the crowd reaction that it was a good one. Dad cursed softly and told me Hunter's ball was on the green, too—just a few inches away from mine.

As we walked toward the green to putt, I couldn't help but think about Birdie. Heatstroke could be serious. I've heard that people die from it sometimes. With Birdie having asthma, who knew what might be happening at the hospital right now?

Then another thought crowded itself into my head. Birdie had her cell phone with her!

"Dad," I suddenly asked, "do you have your cell phone on you?"

"Sure," he said. "Who do you need to call?"

"Nobody," I told him. "When I putt, Birdie puts her cell phone in the hole so I can—"

"I know, I know," Dad said. "I've been watching you. Well, you're not gonna do that anymore."

"What? Why not? I *have* to!" I was in a panic.

"That's not golf," Dad said simply. "In golf, you use skill. You use luck sometimes. But you don't use electronics. You're gonna have to make this putt on your own."

"But I could lose a million bucks, Dad!"

"You win or lose it fair and square."

I was sweating all over by the time we got to the green. Ever since Birdie and I thought of the cell phone trick, I had used it for every putt. I didn't think I could do it without the sound of "Blackbird" coming out of the hole.

"Who's away?" Hunter asked once we reached the green.

In golf, proper etiquette is for the player who is farthest away from the hole to putt first. But Hunter's ball and my ball were almost the exact same distance from the hole, about ten feet.

"We'll flip a coin," said Mr. Ho'okena. "Mr. Bogard, you call it."

"Tails," I said.

"And tails it is."

I figured I would putt first. I wanted to get this thing over with. Also, I figured that if I could sink the putt, it would put a lot of pressure on Hunter to sink his.

"We'll go last," Dad said.

"Dad, why?" I asked.

"If he goes first, he has to read the green," Dad whispered. "I can watch his putt and see how the ball breaks."

It made sense. It hadn't occurred to me that there was an advantage to letting the other guy putt first.

It seemed like it took forever for Hunter and Ronnie to read the green and line up the putt. I was getting impatient.

"He can't figure out which way the ball is going to break," Dad whispered.

"Do *you* know which way it's going to break?" I asked.

"Nope," Dad replied. "I'm glad you called tails."

Finally, Hunter was ready. He and Ronnie whispered back and forth a little, then Ronnie set him up. A hush fell over the crowd. I heard the sound of Hunter's putter tap the ball. A few seconds, and then . . .

"Ooooh!" went the crowd.

"The ball rimmed the cup," Dad told me. "Nice try, though. You make this putt and you win, son."

I walked around the green to get a feel for it. It felt like there was a slight break to the right and a slight downhill slope.

"Okay," Dad whispered, "this is a piece of cake. Ten feet. His ball broke about two inches to the right, and he missed by about an inch on the right side of the hole. So you're gonna have to hit it about three inches to the left side. And you're going downhill a little, so let it roll. But don't leave it short. Got it?"

"Got it."

Dad lined me up and went over to stand behind the hole.

"No pressure, Bogie," somebody cracked as I got myself in position. The crowd laughed.

"You hear the sound of my voice?" Dad asked.

"Yeah."

"You know what to do?" he asked.

"Yeah."

"It's just a putt," Dad said. "Nothin' but a little putt."

Right. It was nothin' but a little *life or death* putt. Nothin' but the most important putt I would ever take. Nothin' but a freaking *million dollar putt*!

I brought my putter back and stroked the ball forward.

Nothing I could do mattered now. It was out of my hands.

"Go, ball!" somebody shouted.

"Keep rolling, baby!" somebody screamed.

Everybody started shouting and yelling and screaming, as if they could influence what the ball did. But at this point, it was all luck and gravity.

And then I heard the sound of the ball rattling into the cup.

Who would think that a silly golf ball falling into a hole would start a riot? But after I nailed that putt, the place went nuts. Everybody was yelling and screaming and taking my picture and slapping me on the back until it was sore. Hunter Lynch came over and shook my hand.

It was like I had won the U.S. Open or something. Mr. Ho'okena gave me a check and this giant trophy that I could barely pick up. I tried to think of a moment in my life that was better than this one. I couldn't come up with anything.

Through it all, in the back of my head, I was thinking about Birdie. She was the one who got me there. She should have been there for the celebration.

They were giving out pizza and cake, but Dad and I left to go visit Birdie in the hospital. It was only a few miles away.

The receptionist at the front desk told us Birdie's room number, and we walked down the hall until we found it. Dad carried the trophy for me. I wasn't sure if Birdie would be awake, but I knew she was as soon as I opened the door.

"Mr. Millionaire!" Birdie shouted.

"Are you okay?" I asked.

"Yeah," Birdie replied. "I got heatstroke. I'll be fine in a few days."

"We heard the news!" somebody else said. "Congratulations!"

It was Birdie's weird parents.

"We'll leave you folks alone for a little while so you can have some privacy," Birdie's dad said. The door opened and closed.

"There must be some yellow-bellied sapsuckers out in the hallway," I cracked.

"You won!" Birdie beamed. "I knew you would."

"*We* won," I told her. "We're a team, remember? You get half."

"Bogie, don't be ridiculous," she said. "You're the golfer. You made the shots."

"I couldn't have made the shots without you," I insisted. "You deserve it."

Birdie started crying. But it wasn't sad crying. It was the kind of crying you do when you're so happy you can't control yourself.

CHAPTER 20

Waiting for This Moment

A COUPLE OF DAYS LATER, while he was eating breakfast, Dad put down his newspaper and called me over.

"Hey, what do you say we go out and shoot a round today?"

"A round of golf?" I asked. I couldn't believe what I was hearing.

"Of course a round of golf!" he said.

"But you said you'd never play again, Dad."

"So I changed my mind."

He pulled his old clubs out of the basement and

wiped the dust and cobwebs off them. We threw our stuff in the back of the truck and drove out to Waikoloa Kings' Course. It's a private course that charges a fortune to play, but Dad and I got in for free because he works there sometimes.

He coached me. As a coach he was great, and as a golfer he was awesome. He showed me a few new tricks, like how to adjust your swing and stance when you're facing uphill or if the terrain slopes to one side. He showed me a trick shot where you turn your club around backward if you're stuck behind a tree and can't hit it the regular way. Dad knew so much about the game.

But the coolest part was that Dad got a golf cart for us. Instead of having to lug our clubs around for miles, we rode in style.

We had just finished the eighth hole when Dad turned to me and said, "Hey, you want to drive?"

"Very funny," I said. "You know I can't drive."

"You can do *anything*," he insisted. "Take the wheel."

It was a big fairway and nobody else was around, so we switched seats and I took over. Dad showed me where the brake and accelerator pedals were. I pushed my foot down and we were off and running.

What a rush! I hope nobody was watching, because they would have thought I was crazy, zigzagging all over the golf course. If I got too close to a tree or something, Dad shouted for me to turn. It was great. I could have driven that thing all day.

As far as the golf went, it wasn't my best round. I shot a 93. Dad shot an 85, and probably would have done a lot better than that if he hadn't taken all those years off from golf. It didn't matter. We had a great time together. After I putted out on the eighteenth hole, he said we should go golfing again sometime soon.

When we got home, we found a note that had been slipped under the front door. Dad read it to me. . . .

You are invited to Waimea School
in Kona tonight at 7:30 P.M.
Please come!

Waimea was the name of Birdie's school. I had never been there. Birdie hadn't mentioned anything going on at her school.

I thought about going over to her house or calling her on the phone and asking what was up, but decided not to. Whatever was happening, she wanted to spring it on me. That was the way she was.

Dad said he would drive me over to Waimea, and offered to stay there with me if I wanted him to. I did. It might be weird going to somebody else's school, you know, not knowing anyone.

"Do you think we should get dressed up?" Dad asked.

"I don't know," I replied. "I have no idea what we're going to."

When we pulled into the parking lot at Waimea, Dad told me there was a sign in front of the school that said there would be a talent show tonight.

"So *that's* it!" I said. "Birdie's going to be in the talent show!"

I remembered when Birdie and I had first met. She was so shy and inhibited that she spied on me, hoping I wouldn't even know she was there. She said she could never learn how to play guitar. She said she was no good at anything. And now she was going to be in a talent show.

I had only taught her those three chords. I wondered what she would play.

Somebody handed us programs and Dad told me that Birdie would be the tenth act. We found seats toward the front of the auditorium. The place must have been crowded. Kids and their parents were buzzing until the principal got on the microphone and asked everybody to quiet down so the show could begin.

The first act was a girl who played something by Mozart on the piano. She was pretty good. The next few were awful. There was a horrible rap song, an even worse heavy metal band, and some kid who called himself a comedian—but his jokes were bombing so badly that he just walked off the stage before his time was up. It was sad. Then three guys in grass skirts and coconut shells on their chests juggled and did a hula dance that cracked up the audience.

Finally, after a few more kids performed, Birdie's name was announced and she came out on the stage. Dad and I applauded and whistled like crazy.

"She's got your old Yamaha," Dad whispered.

The applause died down. I could hear Birdie adjusting the microphone.

"I want to dedicate this song to my boyfriend," she said. "I thought I was doing him a big favor by helping him, but all along he was the one who was helping me."

She plucked the first few notes, and then she started to sing. . . .

Blackbird singing in the dead of night,

Take these broken wings and learn to fly,

All your life,

You were only waiting for this moment to arise.

Blackbird singing in the dead of night,

Take these sunken eyes and learn to see,

All your life,

You were only waiting for this moment to be free.

Blackbird fly,

Blackbird fly,

Into the light of a dark black night. . . .

ABOUT THE AUTHOR

DAN GUTMAN broke 100 once, but he cheated. He is much better at writing books for kids than he is at playing golf. Dan is the author of *The Million Dollar Shot, The Million Dollar Kick*, *The Million Dollar Goal*, and *The Million Dollar Strike*, *Virtually Perfect*, *The Kid Who Ran for President*, *Honus & Me*, and the My Weird School series. Dan lives in Haddonfield, New Jersey, with his wife, Nina, and their two children. If you would like to find out more about Dan or his books, visit his Web site: www.dangutman.com